IN THE DEAD OF WINTER

This Large Print Book carries the
Seal of Approval of N.A.V.H.

COZY IN KANSAS, BOOK 1

In the Dead of Winter

A ROMANCE MYSTERY

Nancy Mehl

THORNDIKE PRESS
A part of Gale, Cengage Learning

GALE
CENGAGE Learning™

Detroit • New York • San Francisco • New Haven, Conn • Waterville, Maine • London

GALE
CENGAGE Learning™

Copyright © 2008 by Nancy Mehl.
Scripture taken from the HOLY BIBLE, NEW INTERNATIONAL
VERSION ®. NIV ®. Copyright © 1973, 1978, 1984 by International Bible
Society. Used by permission of Zondervan. All rights reserved.
Thorndike Press, a part of Gale, Cengage Learning.

LIBRARY OF CONGRESS CATALOGING-IN-PUBLICATION DATA

Mehl, Nancy.
   In the dead of winter / by Nancy Mehl. — Large print ed.
     p. cm. — (A romance mystery cozy in Kansas ; no.1)
   (Thorndike Press large print Christian mystery)
   ISBN-13: 978-1-4104-2484-6 (alk. paper)
   ISBN-10: 1-4104-2484-7 (alk. paper)
   1. Towers, Ivy (Ficticious character)—Fiction. I. Title.
PS3613.E425416 2010
813'.6—dc22   2009051958

Published in 2010 by arrangement with Barbour Publishing, Inc.

To Pastor David Brace, who was the very first person to tell me I could fly. Your belief in me changed my life. To Pastor Rob Rotola, who encouraged me to spread my wings and fly even higher. To my heavenly Father, who gave me wings in the first place. It's all for You.

ACKNOWLEDGEMENTS

Creating a fictional town presents an author with many challenges. My thanks to the following people for helping me to translate Winter Break, Kansas, out of my imagination and onto the printed page. Deputy Sheriff Robert P. (Pat) Taylor. Your help has been invaluable. Bob Slotta, a super guy who deserves the title of "The Twainiac." Henry Sweets, curator of the Mark Twain Boyhood Home and Museum. Darrin W. Figgins, funeral director for Garnand Funeral Home in Hugoton, Kansas. Jinwen Liu. For the lessons in Mandarin. To my family. You are my greatest blessing.

1

I gripped the steering wheel in a desperate attempt to keep my car from sliding on the ice-covered road. My decision to leave the main highway had been a huge mistake. I should have realized that the weather would worsen the closer I got to Winter Break. The fury of the storm outside matched the tempest that raged inside me. I was going back to a place I'd abandoned years ago. A mixture of memories tumbled around wildly inside my head. Some brought back feelings of safety and love. Others reminded me of the person I used to be, the person I'd tried hard to leave behind. I finally eased the car slowly to the shoulder. Should I see the storm as an ominous sign? A warning that I was venturing into dangerous territory?

I held my trembling hands in front of the car's heater, grateful my parents had given me their late-model sedan before taking off for China. The car was much nicer than anything I could afford as a lowly college student. I wasn't worried about it quitting on me, but I was definitely concerned about the worsening weather conditions. I'd narrowly missed two deer that had bounded across the road in front of my car. They'd probably felt safe, shielded by a thick blanket of white. Unfortunately, suddenly finding themselves caught in the glare of my headlights had destroyed their sense of security and frightened them only a little less than it had me. I wasn't sure if they'd heard me scream, but the sound still rang in my ears.

I hit the tuning button on the radio, but the numbers ran wildly up the dial. I was a long way out of Wichita. There was nothing for the tuner to lock onto. How much farther was Winter Break? Because of the blizzard, I couldn't find any familiar landmarks.

Winter Break. Named by wagon trains on their way west, the town was founded as a place of refuge when the strong storms of winter erupted. The location didn't actually provide any special protection; it was simply one of the last stops on the trail before hitting the rocky terrain that would eventually become Colorado Territory. Weary travelers knew that steep mountain trails could easily become final resting places for those caught inside Mother Nature's frozen fury. As they waited in Winter Break for the promise of spring, many turned back, deciding that the promise of gold wasn't worth the struggles they faced from weather, disease, Indians, or fellow pioneers who made their way west by stealing what they could from other nomads. As the years went on, Winter Break became nothing more than an odd spot on the Kansas map. Winter came early and left late there. It seemed comfortable in the small town, choosing to settle in until it was finally defeated by the inevitable encroachment of summer.

I put the car into gear and eased back onto the road. With my high beams on and my speed as close to a crawl as possible, I had only a few feet of visibility. However, there wasn't any other traffic on the road. No one else was foolish enough to be out here.

The slow pace gave me plenty of time to think about Aunt Bitty. My late great-aunt Bitty, that is. It would take me awhile before I could think of her in the past tense. When I was a little girl, I'd called her "Grape Aunt Bitty." To make it easier, she simply became Aunt Bitty.

Bitty was the most alive person I'd ever known. She and I had forged a special bond when I was younger. I'd loved her old secondhand bookstore in Winter Break. I'd spent many summers and winter vacations there, sitting on the hardwood floors, sipping either homemade lemonade or cups of thick hot chocolate topped with melting marshmallows while I read through her collection of gently used classics. *Huckleberry Finn, The Adventures of Tom Sawyer, The Chronicles of Narnia, The Bobbsey Twins, Nancy Drew.* An eclectic assortment to be sure, but the hot summer days and cold winter nights had drifted by on wings of magic, and Bitty's store had been my enchanted castle.

Visits to Winter Break had led to my decision to choose English as my major, over the heartfelt protests of my parents. As I got closer to graduation, uncertainty began to haunt me. What could I possibly do with a degree in English? Become an editor? A teacher? Both noble professions, but for some reason, something else wiggled around inside me. A desire for something I'd never been able to put a name to. Of course, it's very difficult to follow a path laid out in the dark. My only option had been to put my future in God's hands. And I had more than once. Phantom whispers of my mother's voice echoed through the quiet inside the

12

car. "Ivy, every time you worry, you take your situation right out of God's hands. Quit worrying and start trusting!"

Easy for her to say. She and my father had always known exactly what they were meant to do. Running a mission in China had been their goal even before they were married. Although they'd never said it, I was pretty sure the only thing that hadn't gone according to their master plan was me. Mother was thirty when she'd gotten pregnant. All my life, I'd sensed that, although my parents loved me, my existence had derailed their ambitions. Once I was in college, it didn't take them long to sell our home, along with almost all of their possessions, and head to China. I was happy for them, but I couldn't help feeling a little abandoned. It was probably selfish, but it felt odd not having any family nearby. Except, of course, Aunt Bitty.

Something flashed across the windshield, breaking my reverie. Surely it wasn't another deer. I started to press lightly on the brake when a light flickered through the veil of white that surrounded the car. Was it another vehicle? I peered through the snow that blew straight at my windshield while the wipers fought furiously to keep my field of vision clear. There it was again. The light wasn't moving. Could I have finally made it to Winter Break?

As if providing an answer to my question, a sign announcing the city limits appeared on the right side of the road. I could barely make it out, but I didn't really need to. From here, I knew the way.

Three years had passed since I'd been to see my aunt, but I had the strangest feeling I'd left only yesterday. Through the snow, I could make out the sheriff's office right next to the only grocery store in Winter Break. The faded sign reading LABAN'S FOOD-A-RAMA swung violently in the wind-driven snow. The lights were on, signaling that Old Man Tater was still up. Dewey Tater, now in his seventies, had run the Food-a-Rama ever since he was twenty-two, after his father, Laban, died of a heart attack. Dewey stayed in Winter Break to take care of his mother until her death ten years ago. Now he lived here alone. Since he'd never married, the Food-a-Rama would probably close for good after Dewey passed away. His life sounded rather sad, but Dewey was well liked, had a lot of friends, and seemed to be perfectly happy. His sense of humor and even temper had been particularly helpful to us kids when we'd call up the store to ask if "Mr. Tater had any taters for sale," or when Amos Parker stole two bottles of

14

strawberry pop and got caught.

Dewey was known for extending credit to almost everyone in town at one time or another. Most of the folks in Winter Break were farmers. There were lean years and times of bounty. Dewey helped people balance out the ups and downs of their lives, and they loved and trusted him. That's why they had eventually elected him mayor of Winter Break. Not that the mayor had much to do in a town of a little over six hundred people, but it was the thought that counted.

I rounded the first corner of Main Street and found myself in front of Miss Bitty's Bygone Bookstore. True to his word, Amos had turned on the lights. I parked right in front of the entrance. Well, maybe *parked* isn't the right word. *Slid to a stop* is more accurate.

I struggled to open the car door as the wind fought to keep it shut. After finally winning the brief battle, I pushed the trunk button on my key fob. Nothing happened. I hit it again, leaning against the car while my face was pelted with small crystals of ice. The trunk lid was frozen shut, and my suitcases were inside. I pushed on the trunk several times with my gloved hands. After yelling at the resistant lid a couple of times, I finally popped it open. I grabbed my two

15

suitcases and skated toward the bookstore entrance. Amos had promised to unlock the door and turn on the heat. I said a brief prayer of thanks for his efforts. I wasn't in the mood to face another frozen lock.

I twisted the large brass knob and practically fell inside. As the door closed behind me, I heard the familiar sound of Bitty's bell. The tinkling of the little silver bell over the door and the smell of old books and lemon oil threw me headlong into the past. For a moment, I was a ten-year-old girl again, searching the ceiling-to-floor shelves for new worlds and wonderful stories to take me away from the awkwardness of puberty, braces, zits, boys, and the uncertainness of life in general. I leaned against the timeworn door, waiting for Bitty to come around the corner. "Ah, it's my beautiful Ivy," she'd sing out whenever I came to stay. And somehow she always made me feel beautiful, even though I wasn't.

This place had been a sanctuary. My sanctuary. I closed my eyes and breathed it in. I'd almost forgotten how wonderful it was. Bitty had turned this old house into a charming bookstore. Her precious books lined the walls in what used to be the living room. The room beyond that, at one time a combination dining room and kitchen, had been turned into a sitting room for patrons who wanted to cuddle up with a book in one of the mismatched, overstuffed chairs or couches scattered around the room. Bitty's rocking chair sat near the carved stone fireplace in the corner. Tears stung my eyelids. Bitty was really gone, yet something of her remained. The bookstore was still here. And I was here.

I picked up my suitcases and set them down at the bottom of the stairs just to the right of the entryway. Bitty's apartment was nestled above the bookstore on the second floor. I'd stay there until I could finalize the funeral arrangements and settle the estate. Christmas break was a little over a month long. Things would have to be resolved before my next semester began. According to Dewey, Bitty had taken care of almost everything — except what to do with the store. Dewey had informed me when he called to tell me about Bitty's accident that she'd left all her worldly goods to me. I was contemplating what I could possibly do with an old, used-book store, when I heard the door creak open in back of me. The bell tinkled again, and the icy wind swooped in. I turned around to see Amos Parker standing in the doorway.

It had been a long time since we'd seen

each other, but I would have known him in a second. He still had the same turned-up nose, ruffled blond hair, and mischievous grin. The only differences were that he was a little older, and he was wearing a deputy sheriff's uniform. Yep, the boy who stole strawberry pop from the Food-a-Rama now kept the law in Stevens County. Of course, in Winter Break itself, there weren't a lot of dangerous criminals. Mostly loose dogs, cats stuck in trees, and an occasional runaway cow. Oh, and old Odie Rimrucker. Used to be he would get locked up every Friday night for drunk and disorderly. But he was always sober and in church by Sunday morning, remorseful and repentant for his sins. Deputy Sheriff Morley Watson waited every Friday night for Odie to come and turn himself in. When Deputy Watson died of a stroke several years ago, Bitty told me it broke Odie's heart. He swore never to touch another drop of alcohol again. I wondered if his promise had held.

"My goodness, Ivy," Amos said, a smile picking at the corners of his mouth, "you turned out to be very pretty."

"Why, thank you, Amos, but I'm wondering why you sound so surprised."

He laughed. "I'll take the fifth. I doubt there's anything I could say that wouldn't get me in trouble."

"Smart move. And by the way, I don't go by Ivy anymore. I use my middle name, Samantha. Everyone calls me Sam."

His eyebrows arched in surprise. "Sam? I don't know. . . . You've always been Ivy to me. Might be hard to change that now."

Amos peeled off his jacket and gloves and hung them on the ancient wooden coatrack near the door. Then he followed me through the bookstore and into the sitting room. I motioned to a large plush chair near the fireplace while I slid into Aunt Bitty's rocking chair across from him. We sat in front of a crackling fire he had obviously set in anticipation of my arrival.

I shook my head. "Sorry, no choice. I didn't want to live with the name Ivy Towers in the real world. Not many people have my mother's sense of humor. Sam suits me fine. Besides, Ivy was a little girl. I've grown up."

Amos leaned back into the thick cushions of the chair and stared into the dancing flames in the fireplace. "That's too bad. I liked Ivy Towers. She was my friend." He turned his head and gazed into my eyes. "I don't know Sam Towers. I hope she's as caring and compassionate as Ivy."

I smiled. "Oh, she's okay. Maybe a little

more practical, but all in all, no one to fear. I don't think you have anything to worry about."

"Good. I'm relieved."

I thought I saw a shadow of something flicker through his expression. For some reason, it made me feel a little flustered. Amos looked like the same person I'd spent hours with, sharing my deepest secrets, but now there was something harder in his face, a look in his eyes I'd never seen before. Truth was, we'd both changed, and I didn't really know him anymore.

"How long has it been, Ivy . . . I mean Sam?" he asked.

"Well, let me see," I responded, trying to work out the answer in my head. "I haven't been back since before I started college. That's three years. But you left when? A couple of years before that?"

"Yeah, I think so. That makes it somewhere around five years since we've seen each other."

I found that rocking gently back and forth in Bitty's chair in front of the warm, comforting fire made me sleepy. I couldn't stifle a yawn. "Sorry," I said sheepishly.

Amos waved away my apology.

"Didn't you go to live with your dad in Oklahoma?" I asked.

His smile didn't reach his eyes. "Yes, but it didn't work out. I imagined my father to be the answer to all my problems. I was bored living in Winter Break. I thought I would 'find myself' in the big city." He laughed, but it was tinged with a note of bitterness.

"And now you're back here?" I asked, stating the obvious.

This time his smile was genuine. For just a moment, I saw my old friend and confidant. "I finally realized that I couldn't *find* myself in a place I didn't belong. Everything I wanted was here." He looked down, his face flushed. "Well, almost everything."

I wanted to ask him what he meant, but I was exhausted and needed some shut-eye. "Amos, what happened to Bitty? I didn't quite understand from Dewey's phone call."

Amos shook his head, his forehead knit in a frown. "I don't know, S–Sam. Isaac called me at the office. He said he'd found your aunt on the floor — that she'd fallen from her ladder."

"So Isaac still works for her," I said mostly to myself. Isaac Holsapple had been her part-time assistant for as long as I could remember. He was a strange little man who kept to himself but seemed totally committed to Bitty and her bookstore.

21

From my vantage point I could see Bitty's old wooden library ladder. I'd watched her roll back and forth in front of the tallest bookshelves, almost as if it were a part of her. How could she have lost her footing?

"How did she fall? Did the ladder come off the track?" I asked.

"No, it was still connected. I found her lying on the floor next to the ladder. When she fell, she hit her head hard." He looked down at his boots and took a deep breath. "She was already gone when I got here, Ivy."

I didn't bother to correct him again. All I could think of was Bitty lying alone on the floor. "Did she die right away?" I meant to ask this question out loud, but it came out in a whisper.

Amos scooted forward in his chair and reached out to me, closing his hand over mine. "There wasn't any indication that she moved again after she fell, Ivy," he said softly. "She probably died instantly. Actually, she looked quite peaceful. Except for the blood . . ."

"Blood? Why would she bleed if she hit her head on the floor? That doesn't make sense."

Amos frowned and let go of my hand. "I don't think anyone ever said she hit her head on the floor. Maybe you just assumed . . ."

I was confused. "Then what happened?"

"She struck her head on the bottom of the ladder. On the metal fixture that covers the rollers."

Of course. Why was I surprised? The iron hardware that covered the casters jutted out on both sides. "I'm sorry, Amos. That makes sense." I tried to smile but couldn't. I was tired, sad, and disgusted. I didn't want to think about the spot where Bitty's body had been, but my eyes were drawn to it, even though my mind fought the urge. Amos noticed.

"I cleaned it up, Ivy," he said quietly. "You can't tell anything happened there."

A sense of relief and gratitude washed through me. I wasn't sure I could have faced bloodstains. I had other questions, but I was too tired to ask them now. "Thank you, Amos. I really appreciate it. Would you mind if we talked more tomorrow? I'm so exhausted, my brain is fuzzy."

"Of course. I'm sorry." As he stood up, he reached over and patted my shoulder. It felt strange to be so close to him again. "I'll see you tomorrow. You rest. If you need any help making the final arrangements, please let me know. I'm sure you want to wrap things up here and get back to your life."

"I don't know. I'm on break from school. Maybe I'll hang around for a while. Catch up with old friends."

I don't know what I expected, but the look Amos shot me didn't convey his excitement at my intention to spend some time in Winter Break.

"There's not really anything here for you, Sam," he said. "It's been a long time. Town's changed. People change, too. Might be best if you get things squared away and get back to Wichita."

"You . . . you're probably right. We'll see. I'll think about it tomorrow after I get unpacked."

He stood there for a few moments and stared at me. I started to feel a little uncomfortable, but I wasn't sure why.

Finally, he looked away. "I'll call you tomorrow afternoon if I don't hear from you first. Again, if there's anything you need . . ."

"Thank you," I said. "I really appreciate all your help."

He nodded. "You're welcome. Dewey has your keys and some papers he needs to go over with you. And he brought some supplies over. We stocked Bitty's kitchen so you'd have enough food to get you by for a few days."

I smiled my thanks, but without warning, tears filled my eyes. Being back in Winter Break was stirring up my emotions in a way I hadn't expected.

"Everything will be okay," he said, his voice softening a little. "I'll be here for you."

Once again, I saw the face of my old, trusted friend. At first I thought Amos was going to put his arms around me, but then he pulled back, grabbed his coat and hat, and headed for the front door. He glanced back once before leaving. "I'll see you tomorrow, Ivy."

I stood in the bookstore for a few minutes before heading upstairs to Bitty's apartment. I couldn't take my eyes off the library ladder. Two questions swirled around in my head. *How in the world could she have fallen off? And why did Amos Parker want me out of Winter Break?*

2

I awoke Saturday morning to the sound of ice bouncing off the roof. Great. Ice on top of snow. Perfect weather to organize a funeral.

I turned over on my back and stared up at the ceiling. What had I gotten myself into? My mother had offered to fly back from China to take care of her aunt's final arrangements, but I'd told her to stay put, volunteering myself since I was so much closer. It had seemed the right thing to do at the time, even though I hated the idea of returning to this town without Aunt Bitty's being here. Now that I was actually in Winter Break, I felt overwhelmed with the responsibility. Dewey Tater had reassured me over the phone that everything was in good shape and that Bitty had made detailed preparations, but I was still worried. Taking care of her final wishes was important to me. I wanted to give her the kind of send-off she deserved.

I pulled myself up in bed and looked around. The spare bedroom was exactly as it had been the last time I stayed here. In fact, some of my things still adorned the room; my set of Nancy Drew books sat on top of the oak dresser, and my gold-colored jewelry box with its gaudy, fake ruby rhinestones was next to them. The old iron bed gave a familiar squeak as I sat up, and the same brightly colored rag rug lay on the floor next to the bed, waiting to keep my bare feet warm on a cold winter's morning.

I slid my feet into my slippers and padded out into the hallway. After a stop at the bathroom, I entered Bitty's cozy little kitchen. It was waiting for her, ready to begin breakfast and get the day started. I was the intruder, the interloper trying to take her place. But no one else could ever replace Bitty Flanagan — especially me.

Ever since I'd first stepped into the old bookstore, I'd had the strangest feeling of being watched. I felt it strongly at that moment. In my mind, I could see Bitty sitting at her kitchen table, greeting me with a smile as I emerged from my bedroom. "Good morning, Sleeping Beauty," she'd always call out. Last night, I'd kept expecting to see her standing on her library ladder with a book in her hand, saying, "Now, Ivy. I think this book is just the right one for a day like today." Her presence wouldn't be easily exorcised from this place. It was a part of the building . . . part of each of the books lining the walls downstairs . . . part of me.

I stood there in the silence of the morning, wishing she really would appear and tell me this was all just a bad joke, but the only sound I heard was the dinging of frozen drizzle ricocheting off the roof.

As I opened the refrigerator door in search of caffeine, I almost stumbled over a small bowl of water sitting next to another empty bowl. I'd forgotten all about Bitty's cat. Miss Skiffins was named after a character in *Great Expectations.* Where was she? I hadn't heard from her since my arrival the night before. As if on cue, I heard a soft *meow* from behind me.

"Well, hello, Miss Skiffins," I said to the small calico cat that approached me cautiously. "I'm sure you'd rather see your mistress here this morning, but you'll have to put up with me." I rummaged around in the cabinets until I found several cans of cat food. I pulled the top off a can of tuna-flavored rations and dumped the contents into the empty bowl. I was rewarded with a rub against my shins before the hungry animal attacked the smelly offering. The sound of purring filled the small room. It felt good to take care of Bitty's cat. They had been very close friends. It dawned on me that I would have to find Miss Skiffins a home before I left. My brief euphoria skipped away, replaced by a cautionary sense of gloom. This was a small town. What if no one wanted a tiny calico cat?

Just as I located the coffee can, someone knocked on the street-side door downstairs. I looked down at my black sweatpants and pink Shakespeare T-shirt that proclaimed ALL THE WORLD'S A STAGE. Oh well. At least I was covered up. I reached for my hair and ran my hands through it a couple of times. One thing about supercurly hair — you get pretty much the same effect when you hand comb it as you do after several minutes in front of the mirror with a brush and hair gel. Bitty and I had shared more than a love of books. We both had inherited curly dark red hair and bright green eyes.

I patted Miss Skiffins and ran downstairs. I half expected to see Amos standing outside the large oak entry door embedded with thick, etched glass, but instead, it was Old Man Tater. For some reason, seeing him there caused a lump in my throat. Dewey

29

Tater was a big part of Winter Break — and a huge part of my childhood. I unlocked the door and held it open. Dewey stepped inside, his boots tracking in snow and ice. He looked down at the rapidly melting mush on the carpet in front of the door.

"Sorry, Ivy," he said in a voice that sounded like old, dried paper rustling in an invisible breeze.

"Don't worry about it, Dewey." Although I tried to keep my tone steady, the old man peered at me from under his parka hood with a look that told me I hadn't fooled him one little bit. He opened up his arms, and I tumbled unceremoniously into a much-needed bear hug.

"Everything will be okay," he said, his words muffled slightly by the side of my head.

I pulled out of his embrace and smiled up at him. "Sorry. I didn't realize how much I missed Winter Break until I saw you."

He nodded. "Coming home can do that."

I opened my mouth to protest. This wasn't home. Home was . . . To be honest, I wasn't sure where home was. Even though I lived in Wichita, my dorm room was only a temporary place to roost. I certainly hadn't nested.

Dewey hung up his coat. "Thought we'd

go over some of Bitty's arrangements if it's okay." His vivid blue eyes still twinkled with personality and intelligence. Although his hair was grayer, his face more lined, he still had something — a spark of some kind that hadn't diminished one bit.

"Sure. How 'bout some coffee?" I asked. "I was just getting ready to make some."

"Sounds great, Ivy. I brought some paperwork. I'll get everything ready while you get the coffeemaker going."

For the first time, I noticed the aged and battered briefcase he'd brought in with him. Bitty's last requests. A chill ran through me. The idea of hot coffee suddenly sounded even better than it had before.

Dewey ambled toward the sitting room. He put the case on the polished oak table that sat off to one side of the room then grabbed a couple of dark green padded leather chairs that had been pushed up against the far wall. The table had been a meeting spot for many, many book clubs and town meetings over the last forty years. Now the fate of all of Bitty's worldly goods would be decided there.

"I'll get the fire going while you work on that coffee," Dewey said.

I nodded at him and headed for the stairs. I was grateful to have a few minutes to myself. My emotions jumped around frantically inside me like inept circus acrobats. This was supposed to be a quick trip. Check the arrangements for Bitty's funeral. Tie up any loose ends. Go home. But I hadn't thought the situation out very well before leaving Wichita. It wasn't going to be that easy. There was something I hadn't counted on — the attachment I felt to this place. It was much stronger than I'd realized. In fact, my link to Bitty was almost overwhelming. I'd put her, and Winter Break, out of my mind for the past several years. I'd relegated the whole experience to my childhood. After all, I was growing up, putting away childish things. But I was quickly discovering that my link to the past wasn't so easily broken. It was still alive inside me. I just wasn't sure what that meant to me now.

I started the coffee then grabbed a pair of jeans and a sweatshirt from my suitcase. After changing and actually brushing my hair, I felt more like myself. Maybe Ivy would go back into the past where she belonged. Sam needed to be the person in charge now. I hoped she was strong enough to stand against the ghosts of my former life.

I filled two mugs with coffee, grabbed some sugar and creamer, and joined Dewey at the table next to the rapidly growing fire.

After a couple of sips, he pushed some papers toward me. "It's all pretty straightforward," he said. "Bitty left everything to you. All her bank accounts are in your name. Do you remember signing forms about that?"

I nodded. At the time, I'd put my John Henry on everything Mother told me to. She and Daddy knew they wouldn't be nearby if Bitty should pass away suddenly. She was almost seventy at the time, and my parents planned to be in China for a long time. Someone from the family had to be available. Maybe I should have asked a few more questions, but nineteen-year-olds have a lot of things on their minds. It just hadn't seemed important. What a difference a few years could make.

I looked over the bank statements. "There's over twenty thousand dollars in this business account," I said. "How in the world did Bitty make any money in this tiny town?"

Dewey chuckled. "You didn't think she only sold books to people in Winter Break, did you? Your aunt has customers all over the country. In fact, she's sold quite a few books to buyers overseas. She has an excellent reputation for finding valuable, collectible books."

"I don't know what I thought, to be honest," I said. "I guess I figured Bitty sold old books to people who couldn't afford new ones. I knew she had a few special volumes, but I thought they were hers — something she collected for herself."

Dewey's comments reminded me of something. "I found a couple of boxes of books by her desk. They've both been opened, but it doesn't look as if they've been gone through. Must be a shipment she got in but didn't have time to unpack."

"I'm sure that's exactly what it is." Dewey cleared his throat and frowned at me. "Miss Bitty's Bygone Bookstore was much more than discarded books, Ivy. Your aunt was an expert on rare books. She could find 'em and sell 'em. A lot of people benefited from her expertise. You should be proud of her."

Yes, I should have been. I also should have shown more interest in what Bitty did, but my time in the bookstore had been spent on myself and my own enjoyment. I felt ashamed. I hadn't given Bitty the respect or attention she'd deserved. Now I'd never have the chance.

Dewey shoved several new papers toward me. "You own the bookstore outright since your name is on the title. Also, all the contents are yours." He frowned. "Somewhere there's a list of individual items she wanted her friends to have, but I'm not sure where it is. It's not a legal document, just something she kept around here. I'd look through her desk for it. Even though everything belongs to you, you'll want to honor her wishes. When you find that list, let me know. I'll help you match the people to the things. Might be some folks mentioned that you don't know."

"Okay. I'll look for it a little later."

"Bitty didn't write down anything in particular for your mother. She knew you would make certain she got whatever she wanted." He shrugged. "Bitty tried to give her some of your great-grandmother's things several years ago, but your mother turned them down. Since your grandmother, Bitty's only sister, had already passed, she felt your mother should have some of the family heirlooms."

"That doesn't surprise me," I said. "My mother's only goal in life was to go to China. Before she left, she got rid of almost all of her own possessions. She doesn't seem to value family history much." I could hear the resentment in my voice. I wondered if Dewey noticed it. If he did, he didn't give any indication.

"She may change her mind someday, Ivy. You protect a few of Bitty's things for her, okay?"

"I'll try." I was wondering where in the world I was going to store "Bitty's things." I didn't even have enough storage for "my things," sparse as they were.

Dewey picked up his coffee mug and took a sip. "Many a morning I sat here with your aunt, drinking her coffee and talking about our lives. I'm going to miss that." His eyes grew misty, and he swiped at them with the back of his hand.

"You and Bitty were friends for a long time, weren't you, Dewey?"

His gaze became dreamy. "Yes, a long, long time," he said. "She was my best friend."

I waited a few moments before saying anything else. I didn't want to interrupt his private thoughts. When he reached for his cup again, I asked, "What am I supposed to do with the bookstore, Dewey? Is there anyone in Winter Break who might want to buy it?"

He smiled and shook his head. "I doubt it. Most people here already have their niches carved out. I don't think many Winter Break people understand this place." His forehead wrinkled in thought. "Well, except for Lila Hatcher."

"Lila Hatcher? I don't know the name."

He leaned back in his chair. "Lila and your aunt were pretty close. Maybe she spoke of her to you? She was teaching Lila all about old books."

"Oh yes. Now that you mention it, I do remember something about that." What I remembered was the feeling of guilt I'd had when Bitty talked about her new friend who shared her interest in literature. I used to be the person Bitty talked to about her latest TBR pile. *TBR* stood for *to be read.* At one time, my aunt and I kept each other updated on our lists, sometimes changing them because of suggestions from each other. Obviously, Lila had taken my place.

"Lila moved here a couple of years ago. Lives in the big Biddle house on Oak," Dewey said.

"The Biddle house? What happened to Cecil and Marion?"

Dewey grinned. "Don't look so worried. They moved to Florida. Cecil's arthritis needed a warmer climate."

"I'm glad they're okay. They were such a nice couple. Marion always made candy apples for us kids on the Fourth of July."

Dewey's eyes crinkled with amusement. It was obvious his face was used to wrinkling that way. The deep lines around his eyes spoke of his easygoing, happy nature. "I remember those apples. Wasn't just you kids who were crazy about 'em."

"Why do you think this Lila woman might be interested in the bookstore?"

Before answering, Dewey cleared his throat and took another sip of coffee. "I didn't say I thought she'd be interested. I said she was someone who might understand it. Lila spent quite a bit of time here. She and Bitty were good friends. Of course, Bitty was friends with everyone. She took her Bible seriously. She didn't believe in gossip, and she always tried to think the best of every person. I can't tell you how many times she quoted the verses in First Corinthians about love. If someone had set Miss Skiffins on fire and roasted marshmallows over her, your aunt wouldn't have had an unkind word to say."

It was my turn to laugh. "That might be pushing it a little, even for Aunt Bitty."

Dewey grinned. "Okay. But you get my drift."

"I never realized that you and Bitty were so close," I said. "I'm glad."

A hint of sadness shone in his eyes. "I'll miss her a lot, Ivy. But I know where she is, and I know I'll join her there soon. I keep my mind focused on that. It's how I make it from day to day. 'The goodness of God gives me strength.' "

"I remember Pastor Taylor saying that same thing many times." I'd always enjoyed attending Faith Community Church in Winter Break. It was smaller than our big church in Wichita, but I loved the family feeling there. For many people in Winter Break, church was the center of almost everything they did. "That reminds me. I need to talk to him about the service. It's Saturday already. We don't want to have the funeral on Sunday. I guess Monday would be best."

"Sounds okay. You don't have to rush it, though, Ivy. You set it at a time that will work for you."

I'd intended to ask Dewey to call me Sam when we first sat down at the table, but for some reason, I couldn't do it now. I was Ivy to him, and for the first time in a long time, it felt okay. "I doubt that Mr. Buskin would want me to wait too long," I said. "I mean, don't we need to get Bitty buried as soon as possible?"

Dewey looked startled. "You knew she was cremated, didn't you?"

It was my turn to look surprised. "What? No. I had no idea."

Dewey stood up and walked over to the fireplace. He grabbed a poker and jabbed at the logs. The flames flared up again, sending a rush of warmth my way. "She decided on cremation after she found out how much less it would cost than regular burial. Your aunt didn't like spending money on herself. She decided this would give her more to pass on to you — and be less of a bother." He put the tool back in its holder and turned around. "And maybe," he said mildly, "she wasn't sure how fast someone could get here if something happened to her. She knew your mother would be out of the country, and she didn't know if you would be available."

His words stung me. Bitty hadn't trusted her family to come if something happened to her. Tears filled my eyes.

"Now don't you go feeling bad, Ivy. Bitty knew you loved her. She thought the world of you. And she was so proud, especially with you studying English in college. She always suspected she might have had something to do with your interest in English and literature."

"She was right," I said, dabbing at my eyes with the side of my hand. "She definitely passed along her love of the written word."

Dewey sat down again. "That's good to

hear. That's mighty good to hear."

"Bitty certainly seems to have everything arranged, Dewey," I said, glancing through the paperwork. "I know her well enough to understand that she felt the need to have all her ducks in a row, but from what you told me on the phone, she finalized several things in the past couple of months. Do you find that a little odd?"

He shrugged. "You know your aunt prided herself on having everything planned out as much as possible. She started making her final arrangements when she was still in her sixties. She wanted everything to go off without a hitch when she met her Maker." He looked off into space for a moment. "It did seem a little strange to me that she got so focused on all kinds of little details just lately. It was almost as if she knew she wasn't going to be around much longer." He smiled and shook his head. " 'Course, that was Bitty. She spent her life trying to be prepared for everything that might happen. That was one of her few weaknesses. And those lists she made. I swear, she would have submitted a list to the Lord for every day of her life, if He'd been interested. I told her that He might have a few ideas of His own, and she should let Him have a say so every once in a while. She tried, she really did, but it was a struggle." He grinned at me. "Never saw anyone so organized. I'll bet she's got the heavenly host on a pretty tight schedule already."

Aunt Bitty and I were obviously more alike than I'd realized. I was a list person, too, although I wasn't as obsessed as my aunt was. I felt better when everything was mapped out ahead of time. I wasn't about to confess my Achilles' heel to Dewey Tater, so I just nodded as though I agreed with him.

Dewey straightened up. "So that's about it," he said. "There's a small insurance policy in here made out to you. You'll have to contact them yourself. You can proceed with the rest of this as if it's yours, 'cause it is. Again, I'd look in her desk for that list of things set aside for some of her friends. This stuff she kept in a box with instructions that I was to open it and give it to you if something happened. I've done that. She probably wouldn't have cared if I'd gone through her desk, but since she didn't tell me to, I felt . . . I don't know." He shrugged his shoulders. "I didn't want to breach her privacy. Or yours."

"Thanks, Dewey. But I think you're right. She wouldn't have minded."

"Oh, before I forget." He reached into the

pocket of his jeans. "Here are all of her keys." He held up a key ring. "This is to the front door," he said, pointing to a square, gold-colored key. He pushed it out of the way and held up another one. "This is to the back door." He let that drop. "This is the key to Isaac's apartment next door, and this is to the valuables box these papers and checkbooks came out of. I put that box back in her closet where she kept it. There are a few other keys I don't recognize — you'll have to find out where they fit. And this one," he said gently, "is to your aunt's desk." His gaze moved to the antique cherrywood desk in the corner of the main room. I could still see my aunt sitting there, holding court as the queen of Miss Bitty's Bygone Bookstore. I knew Dewey could envision her, too.

We were silent for a few seconds, each lost in our own thoughts. Dewey reached out and touched my arm. "You let me know if you need anything, okay? Why don't I walk you over to Buskin's Funeral Home?"

I nodded. "That would be nice. I think I'd like to unpack, maybe take a shower before we go."

Dewey nodded. "I understand. Should I come back and get you around eleven? We can have a quick lunch at the Redbird before we see Elmer."

Ruby's Redbird Café. With everything else happening, I'd forgotten all about it. My mouth started to water just at the mention of Winter Break's only restaurant. Run by Ruby Bird for over thirty years, it was the town's most important attraction, even drawing visitors from neighboring cities. In fact, once in a while, old customers came back to see Ruby after moving across the country. If their travels brought them within two hundred miles of the Redbird Café, it meant a quick trip to Winter Break.

Ruby made breakfast plates that could feed three people: eggs fried just right with crispy edges and soft middles; homemade sausage with just a touch of spice; buttery hash browns; fried apples; creamy grits; and hot, fresh cinnamon bread that seemed to melt in your mouth. Her homemade soups were legend, and her pies had been known to save marriages, heal broken hearts, and bring families back together.

Almost everyone in town knew the story of Dolly and Pete Palavich, who had once owned a farm just outside town. Dolly had packed her bags, determined to find a man who appreciated her, when Pete showed up with one of Ruby's shoofly pies. Although it was hard for Pete to tell Dolly how much he loved her, the pie did the job for him. Dolly decided to stay. They were married for fifty-one years before Pete passed away.

But the thing Ruby was really famous for was her one-pound cheeseburgers. Ruby's Redbird Burger was something you'd never taste anywhere on this earth except at the Redbird Café. Although she wouldn't tell anyone her secret recipe, most of the towns-folk knew she added minced onions and jalapeños to the beef, along with some extra-sharp New York cheddar cheese stuck in the middle somehow. Then she grilled them and covered them with more cheddar cheese, lettuce, tomato, grilled onions, and mustard. No one ever, ever asked Ruby to add ketchup to her burgers. To Ruby, adding ketchup to a hamburger was a sin, pure and simple.

A lot of people had tried to recreate the Redbird Burger, but without success. Ruby had a secret ingredient. Something she kept to herself. All anyone could hope for was that before Ruby passed away, she'd reveal the mystery to someone she trusted. The thought that the Redbird Burger could be lost forever was too much for love-struck burger connoisseurs to comprehend. It was a major concern for the citizens of Winter Break, even prompting town meetings

45

designed to wrestle the top-secret information from the obstinate restaurateur. So far, all strategies had failed miserably.

Ruby found the whole "Redbird Burger controversy," as it was called, quite humorous. She loved to tease her customers by claiming loudly to anyone who would listen that she planned to "go to my grave with the very last Redbird Burger clutched in my cold, dead hand."

Needless to say, Redbird Burger aficionados didn't find it the least bit funny.

After happily agreeing to Dewey's proposal, I saw him to the door and was on my way back upstairs when my gaze fell on Bitty's desk. Curiosity got the best of me, and I decided to see what was inside.

First I moved the two boxes of newly arrived books into the corner near the bookshelves. I'd go through them later. It took me a few moments to actually sit down on Bitty's antique swivel desk chair. In my whole life, I'd never seen anyone but my aunt sit in this chair. If she had been a queen, her desk chair would have been her throne. Unfortunately, Bitty had moved to another kingdom, and I had temporarily taken her place. As I slid the key Dewey had given me into the locked desk drawer, it hit me for the first time that this wasn't actually Bitty's desk anymore. It was mine. Frankly, the whole idea hit me like a slap in the face. I gazed around the bookstore. It was all mine. I'd never really owned anything before. Even the house I grew up in had belonged to someone else. Now I lived in a dorm room as a temporary occupant. A strange feeling came over me. For just a moment, I felt an odd sense of belonging to something. But as quickly as the thought came, I pushed it away. This was Bitty's world. My world was back in Wichita, studying English. I forced myself to put my focus back on the task at hand.

I unlocked the deep top drawer of the desk and pulled it open. There were quite a few papers inside, as well as several large bound books with the word *Accounts* on the outside. I pulled the top one out and leafed through it. It was just as Dewey had said. Rows and rows of names and transactions filled the pages. Bitty had customers all over the planet. Although most of the addresses were in the States, several entries referenced overseas addresses.

I put the book on top of the desk, intending to spend more time going over it later. Then I pulled out a folder that housed a stack of papers. Most of the information seemed to be work related, until I came upon a large envelope with the words *Last Will and Testament* written on it. Inside were several handwritten sheets. Glancing over the first several pages, I saw that Bitty had written down exactly what Dewey had already told me. She wanted everything she owned turned over to me. A letter-sized envelope slid out from the middle of the papers and fell to the floor. I leaned over to pick it up and saw that my name was written on it. A letter left for me from Bitty. My throat constricted with emotion. I put the envelope on top of the desk next to the account book. I would read it later when I had time to give it the proper attention it deserved.

At the bottom of the various pages, I found what I'd been looking for: a list of items with a person's name written next to each one. There were eight names on the list. Isaac Holsapple, Dewey Tater, Ruby Bird, Alma Pettibone, Pastor Taylor, Amos Parker, Dr. Lucy Barber, and Lila Hatcher. I didn't know Dr. Barber, but I'd heard about the young doctor who'd moved into the area a couple of years earlier. If I remembered correctly, she lived in nearby Hugoton. I could tell that Bitty had actually started the list quite some time ago. A couple of the names were crossed off and added again at the bottom. She must have changed her mind about what she wanted to leave them.

Each corresponding item willed to the mentioned individuals appeared to be a book or a set of books. That made sense. Books were Bitty's most treasured possessions. I put all the other pages back into the large envelope and laid the list on top of Bitty's book of accounts that was on top of the desk next to the envelope with my name on it. The rest of the papers went back into the drawer, which I locked. At some point I would go through everything more carefully, but right now there wasn't much time left to shower and get ready to meet Dewey. Maybe I would get a chance later tonight. Besides, I could clearly hear a Redbird Burger calling my name.

I stared at the envelope with my name on it for a few moments before I went upstairs. I had to assume that Bitty had made all her final arrangements because at her age, she wanted to be prepared, but being this organized still seemed rather unusual. Could she really have sensed that her time on earth was drawing to a close? But how could that be? I felt a sudden chill that had nothing to do with the temperature outside.

A hot shower tends to make everything

seem better somehow. After showering and changing clothes, I was ready to take on a Redbird Burger with gusto. I checked my watch on the way downstairs — twenty minutes to eleven. I had time to read Bitty's letter while I waited for Dewey to arrive.

The accounts book was where I'd left it, along with the list of books and recipients. The letter from my aunt was still there, but it had been moved. It now sat on the edge of the desk, with a message scribbled on it next to my name. I picked it up and read: *Please don't leave town. Bitty was murdered. Don't let her killer go free!*

3

A little after eleven, Dewey and I were safely tucked into a booth at the Redbird Café. I thought Ruby was going to lose her ever-present white blond wig at the sight of me coming through her front door. "Why, Ivy Towers," she screeched. "Where in blue blazes have you been keeping yourself? It's about time you came home!"

Ruby was well into her seventies. For as long as I could remember, she had sported a platinum hairpiece in the style of Marilyn Monroe. I had to believe that after all these years, it wasn't the very same wig. She must be down to the great-great-granddaughter of the original by now. It looked absolutely atrocious — but it was Ruby. I couldn't imagine her without it. Ruby was larger than life. Her choice of headgear matched her eccentric personality.

Longtime Winter Break residents knew that Ruby's boisterous behavior hid a secret heartache. Ruby had first come to town in her twenties, a young bride with a new baby. Her husband, Elbert, brought his family to western Kansas to help run his uncle Leonard's farm. Leonard had suffered a stroke that eventually proved fatal. After his death, Elbert, Ruby, and baby Bert stayed on, turning the place into one of the most successful dairy farms in this part of the country. But in the sixties, disaster struck. Elbert was hit by lightning while rounding up cows. He died instantly. Ruby and fifteen-year-old Bert tried to run the farm alone, but it proved to be too much for the diminutive widow and her young son. Several of their neighbors pitched in and offered their help, but with their own farms to run, they weren't able to give the Birds enough assistance to keep going.

Then one day when Bert was only sixteen, he disappeared. Most people in town believed he'd run away, tired and discouraged from trying to fill his daddy's shoes. Ruby was heartbroken. Eventually, she sold the farm and used the money to open the Redbird Café.

The story of the missing Bert Bird remained one of Winter Break's longest-running legends. I'd heard most of the speculation, which ran from the possible to the ridiculous: Bert ran away and became a hippie, showing up in a movie about Woodstock; Bert ran away and joined the circus; Bert became a famous movie producer in Hollywood; Bert was murdered and his ghost still haunts the peach tree groves down by Winter Break Lake; and my favorite — Bert went searching for the much-ballyhooed Lost Gambler's Gold, supposedly buried by a wealthy gambler on his way back from California. Legend had it that he was attacked and killed by Indians not long after hiding the booty he'd won from unlucky gold miners. His treasure was supposedly buried somewhere in Winter Break. The treasure carried a curse, and the hapless Bert had fallen prey to the spirit of the long-dead adventurer. Kids in Winter Break still told stories about the ill-fated gambler reaching out from beneath the ground and calling, "Where's my gold? Do you have it?" then grabbing them around the ankles. The tale had caused many a sleepless night for the town's young people.

After ordering two Redbird Burgers and jawing with Ruby for a while, Dewey and I made small talk while we waited for our gastronomic Redbird adventure to arrive. I wanted to tell him about the odd message written on Bitty's envelope, but to be honest, I wasn't certain if I should. Normally, Dewey would be my first choice as a confidant, but I needed some time to think. The note wasn't geared to frighten me. It appeared to be written by someone who really believed Bitty was murdered. I wanted time to think the situation through. Then I would formulate a plan and decide who I should tell — and who I shouldn't.

Dewey was saying something about Alma Pettibone at the post office. I shook off thoughts about Ruby and Bert and forced myself to concentrate on Dewey.

"Then she placed cherry bombs in every single postal box. When they blew up, it was quite a sight. The whole town watched the old post office take off straight into space. I hear it's still circling the earth."

My confused expression caused Dewey to chuckle. "Oh, you're back. I've been talking nonsense for quite a while. Where have you been?"

I shook my head, mortified by my lack of attention. "I'm sorry, Dewey. I have a lot on my mind, what with Bitty and the bookstore. . . ."

He reached over and touched my hand. "I know that, Ivy. I understand. Sorry I teased you."

His compassionate response made me feel

ashamed that I had harbored any mistrust toward him. I started to tell him about the note, but before I could get the words out, Ruby showed up with our hamburgers. The things were so big they were frightening. The aroma took me back to my childhood. In Winter Break, eating an entire Redbird Burger was the dividing line between childhood and the mysterious world of adults. Once you finished one of Ruby's famous Redbird Burgers, life changed. Other kids looked at you with new respect. Even now, as Ruby delivered her culinary masterpiece, a hush fell over the diner. I wasn't sure, but I thought I saw a man in the corner remove his cap.

"You eat up, honey," Ruby hollered as she set the monstrosity in front of me. "You need some meat on those bones!"

I had no plans to go anywhere near a scale for at least a week after this meal. It would take that long for my "bones" to recover from the shock they were about to receive.

Dewey bent his head and said a short prayer, which made me feel a little better. At least now I had some heavenly protection. It took awhile to figure out how to pick the thing up, but when I did, I chomped down, waiting for what I knew was coming. And it did. I'm not sure what the Lord plans to serve at the Marriage Supper of the Lamb, but I won't be surprised if the table is laid out with Ruby's Redbird Burgers.

After a few minutes of chewing and swallowing, I finally remembered where I was — and that I still had a problem. Dewey seemed to come back to himself, too. The glassy-eyed look that is normal during the enjoyment of a Redbird Burger cleared a little from Dewey's expression, and he smiled at me.

"Does it taste the way you remembered?" he asked, a little grease dribbling down his chin.

I shook my head. "I think it's even better. This has to be why some people never leave Winter Break. They're addicted to Ruby and her cooking."

Dewey grinned. "You're probably right."

I was about to the halfway point, so I put the burger down to rest a little before approaching the second stretch. Maybe my mind was clouded with hamburger grease, but I found myself saying, "Dewey, do you think there's anything strange about the way Aunt Bitty died? I mean, she was almost one with that ladder, she was so used to it. Don't you find it odd that she could fall off like that?"

Dewey, who was also resting for the final

sprint in the Ruby race, frowned at me. "I guess I was surprised a little, Ivy. But obviously something went wrong and she fell. There's no other explanation." He stared at me for a moment. "Sometimes it's best to accept things and go on, even if it's hard."

For some reason his comment struck me as being somewhat callous, but Dewey Tater wasn't an insensitive person. In fact, just the opposite. Without thinking it through, I blurted out, "So it never occurred to you that something else might be behind her accident?"

Dewey's face turned so white it scared me. "Ivy Towers, why in the world would you say something like that?" He lowered his voice so no one in the restaurant could hear him. "There's not a soul in this town that would hurt Bitty. For goodness' sake. I hope you don't repeat that to anyone else."

I'd upset Dewey. The realization made my stomach a little queasy. Or maybe it was the Redbird Burger, but whatever it was, I felt bad. Dewey was someone I respected. It was obvious I wouldn't be able to share my suspicions with him, and I certainly couldn't tell him about the message left on the envelope. I flashed him an apologetic smile. "You're right, Dewey. Sorry. I guess living in the big city puts ideas in your head. I

57

shouldn't have brought it up. Let's forget it."

He nodded, but his face still held a shadow of suspicion — or something else. I would have given the second half of my burger to know what he was thinking. Well, maybe not. But there was definitely more to Bitty and Dewey than met the eye. All of a sudden, something Dewey said earlier today about having coffee in the mornings with Bitty, along with a few of his other comments, clicked on a light in my brain.

"Dewey. You and my aunt — were you . . ." I couldn't quite find the words.

Dewey hung his head for a moment. When he looked up, there were tears in his eyes. "I loved your aunt with all my heart, Ivy. And she loved me, too. We even talked about getting married."

"I had no idea, Dewey. That's wonderful." I reached over and touched his arm. "I'm so happy she had you in her life. I wish she'd lived long enough to marry you."

He pulled a handkerchief out of the pocket of his shirt and blew his nose. "I do, too, Ivy. But wedding or not, we loved each other. That's the most important thing."

"Dewey, please don't take this wrong, but I'm surprised you and Bitty were so close. I knew you were friends, but you haven't seemed all that upset about her death."

"You mean because I'm not constantly bawling my eyes out in front of you?" He shook his head. "I miss her every second. It hurts. A lot." His eyes locked on mine. "But I truly believe that Bitty is alive and waiting for me. And I don't think we'll be apart much longer. I have my gaze set on heaven." He stared somewhere past me — looking at something only he could see. " 'Where your treasure is, there will your heart be also.' " He smiled at me. "I guess I'm looking to my treasure, Ivy. That's all."

I was moved by his words and desperately wanted to ask more questions. Like how long had he and my aunt been in love? Why didn't they marry years ago? Unfortunately, this wasn't the time to get that personal. Besides, there'd been enough revelations for one morning. I stared at the rest of my hamburger and stirred up all the courage I had to continue my burger battle. Before I could begin round two, a voice cut through my beef-dazed stupor.

"Excuse me. Are you Ivy Towers?"

I looked up into eyes the color of deep blue evening skies and a smile so warm and brilliant I felt momentarily blinded. Okay, maybe I'm being a little overly dramatic, but this was one good-looking guy.

I responded brilliantly. "Huh?"

His smile grew wider. "I'm looking for Ivy Towers."

"I–I'm Ivy Towers." I looked at Dewey, who nodded to confirm the fact that I was who I said I was. "Can I help you?"

"May I sit down a minute?"

I bobbed my head up and down, which he obviously took as a yes.

"I'm sorry to interrupt your lunch."

Lunch? What lunch? Even though I wouldn't have believed it, Ruby's Redbird Burger had just taken second place in my heart. This guy was something. Tall, his dark hair just long enough to be romantic without being scruffy, black leather coat and gloves, and the kind of features you usually see only on the front of trashy romance novels. Not that I would know anything about that, of course.

"That's okay," I managed to squeak out. "What can I do for you?" I had a list of possibilities forming in my mind, but I was pretty sure his suggestion wasn't going to be among them.

He handed me a business card that I took without removing my eyes from his face. "I'm Noel Spivey. I did business with your aunt from time to time. I heard she passed away. I'm terribly sorry."

"Why, thank you," I said, grateful to have finally remembered the English language. "That's kind of you to say. Are you from around here, Mr. Spivey?"

And yes. I already saw the problem. Ivy Spivey. But I could overcome it. I'd been calling myself Sam for many years now. The name change would force me to bury Ivy for good.

And no, I wasn't jumping too far ahead. It's good to get things lined up as soon as possible. Saves headaches later.

"Actually, I live in Denver."

"You drove quite a ways in some pretty bad weather to get here," Dewey interjected. "What's so important?"

I glanced over at Dewey in surprise. His tone was a little rude, and that wasn't like him.

"Well, I'd like a chance to talk to Ms. Towers about that," Noel said. "I deal in rare books. I thought she might be interested in selling her aunt's inventory." He flashed another charming smile. "I hope it doesn't seem inappropriate — my coming here so soon after Miss Flanagan's death. I could have called sometime next week, but I really wanted to attend her funeral if possible. I had a lot of respect for her."

"No," I said after sending a warning look

to Dewey. "I think it's very thoughtful. I appreciate it."

Dewey scowled but kept his mouth shut.

"Thank you, Ms. Towers. Now I need to find a place to stay. Are there any motels in Winter Break?"

I started to tell him that the closest motel would be in Hugoton, but Dewey interrupted me before I could get the words out.

"No motel here," he said grudgingly, "but I heard that Sarah Johnson has a room for rent. She has a clean home and she's a good cook. You'd be quite comfortable there."

Noel looked relieved. "Thanks for the information. I would really rather not get out on those roads again. It's pretty icy. If you could just point me in the right direction . . ."

Dewey told him how to get to Sarah's house while I tried to look him over without being too obvious. I really wished I'd taken the time to put some makeup on before I left the bookstore. It pays to remember that what your mother told you about clean underwear works with makeup, too. I'd certainly learned my lesson.

As Noel got ready to leave, he held out his hand. "Thank you for your time, Ms. Towers."

"Please. Call me Sam," I said.

He looked confused. "I thought your name was Ivy."

I shook my head and gave him my best smile. I hoped that mutilated shreds of Redbird Burger weren't stuck between my teeth. "I was known as Ivy when I was a child. My name is actually Ivy Samantha. I go by Sam."

"Then Sam it is." He held my hand a little longer than necessary. I didn't fight it. "Do you have a time set for your aunt's service yet?"

I explained that I was on my way to make those arrangements and offered to call him with the information later in the afternoon. He left with the telephone number of the bookstore and my promise to meet with him about my aunt's books after the funeral.

I watched him walk out of Ruby's, as did every other female in the place. I put his card in my coat pocket then turned my attention back to Dewey and the rest of my hamburger. For some reason, the added pounds that were waiting to jump onto my hips seemed more important than they had just a few minutes earlier. As I pushed my plate away, I could swear I heard a sigh of disappointment sweep through the room. I noticed that Dewey was still sullen.

"What's the matter? You seem upset," I said.

He shook his head. "I don't know. Something about that guy." Dewey leaned back and crossed his arms over his chest. "How'd he know about Bitty dying? Only place it's been reported is in the Hugoton newspaper. Seems unlikely that a guy who lives in Denver would be reading the *Hugoton Gazette.*"

It was a good question. I added it to the growing list of questions I had about my aunt's death. As I watched Dewey finish his Redbird Burger, I realized that my list was getting pretty long. I was becoming more and more suspicious about Aunt Bitty's accident.

Suddenly, Winter Break, Kansas, didn't feel quite so friendly.

4

Dewey and I waddled over to Buskin's Funeral Home after turning down Ruby's offer of hot apple pie to top off our Redbird Burgers. I couldn't find the words to explain to her how impossible it was to put one more ounce of food into my already-suffering stomach, so I just shook my head and headed for the door. Ruby's partial deafness kept her from hearing Dewey mumble something about not having hollow legs.

As we walked out, she screeched, "I'm fryin' up a mess of fresh catfish tonight. Mashed potatoes whipped with cream and butter. Homemade biscuits and —" Thankfully, Dewey closed the door behind us, cutting off the rest of Ruby's cholesterol-laden proclamation. At that moment, I wasn't certain I would ever be able to eat again.

It was so cold outside, I felt that I'd walked smack into an open freezer. The ice and snow had finally stopped falling, but the clouds that drifted overhead looked as though they still had some business to attend to.

Dewey and I didn't talk on our way to Buskin's. It was only a couple of blocks away, and we weren't tempted to open our mouths since any conversation might slow us down. Survival instinct had kicked in. Continual movement was our only defense against becoming permanent popsicles.

When we reached Buskin's, Dewey, ever the gentleman, held the door open for me. Frankly, I wouldn't have blamed him if he'd run inside and left me to fend for myself. Self-preservation is a powerful instinct. Once we stepped into the main lobby, I had to stand still a few seconds just to soak in the surrounding warmth and get my muscles moving again.

"Why, there you are, Miss Ivy."

I elevated my frozen eyeballs a little to see Elmer Buskin peering at me from beneath his bushy gray eyebrows. His ever-present smirk was properly glued in place. For a man whose life was spent dealing with the dead, he always seemed suspiciously happy about it.

"He–hello, Mr. B–B–Buskin. It–it's b–been a long t–time." I was pretty sure my teeth would stop chattering at some point. If not, future conversations with me were going to require a lot of patience.

"Yes. Yes, it has, Miss Ivy. And now we meet again under these dark circumstances." His bloodshot eyes didn't match his black funeral director suit, but they did go very well with his bright red bow tie. Most people in town suspected that Elmer Buskin kept a little nip in his office and indulged from time to time. As kids, Amos and I used to tell anyone who would listen that he drank embalming fluid. When Aunt Bitty heard it, she gave us both a good talking to, expounding on the evils of gossip and "bearing false witness." It hadn't stopped us from saying it, but at least we felt guilty about it every time we did. That surely counted for something.

"Please. Let's go to my office where we can talk," Elmer said. Everything about Elmer Buskin was odd, from the way he looked to the way he acted. But one of his strangest features was his voice. Although he tried to sound appropriately funereal, his high-pitched voice and pronounced speech impediment caused him to sound like a cross between Darth Vader and Tweety Pie. Dewey and I followed him through the overly ostentatious lobby. Faded red brocade wallpaper accented the darkened oriental rugs. The crystal chandelier, which still swung slightly from the wind that had swept inside when we opened the front doors, was decorated with dust and cobwebs. Buskin's Funeral Home was a second-hand Rose dressed up in high-society cast-offs. Unfortunately, her garments were threadbare and worn. Dewey had told me that Elmer could barely keep his head above water. Most Winter Break people picked one of the two funeral homes in Hugoton when they faced a death in the family. The facilities were much nicer and more modern. Besides, some folks were a little afraid of Elmer Buskin. Whether it was the man himself, the rumors spread by imaginative kids conjuring up ghost stories on dark, stormy nights, or simply Elmer's occupation, most people kept their distance. Except, of course, my aunt Bitty. She would have viewed giving her mortal remains to a funeral home outside of Winter Break as extreme disloyalty, bordering on rudeness. And Aunt Bitty was never, ever rude.

Elmer's office was just as shabby as the lobby. Dewey and I sat down on two burgundy Queen Anne–styled chairs positioned in front of Elmer's desk. They looked old enough to have actually held the derriere of the long-dead regent herself. The finish was worn off the arms, and the legs of my chair wobbled badly. I had to grab the edge of the plywood desk to steady myself. Dewey looked a little concerned about the noises coming from underneath him. He was a big man, and the creaks and moans emanating from the ancient chair were dire warnings of impending collapse. Finally, he stood up, professing to be tired of sitting and having the need to stretch his legs.

Elmer proceeded as if he hadn't noticed anything wrong. "I want to tell you how sorry I am about your aunt," he said to me. "She was a wonderful person. So kind. And such a pretty woman." Except it came out more like "tuch a pitty woman."

"Thank you, Mr. Buskin," I said. "I appreciate everything you've done for Aunt Bitty. Is there anything we need to do besides make arrangements for the memorial service?"

"No. Everything else was taken care of by your aunt. She prepaid for all the services we have provided."

"And I understand that she chose cremation?"

He nodded. "Yes, she did. I still remember what she said to me about it. 'Just return me to dust, Elmer. I'm not worried about it. God will know where I am. That's all that counts.' "

It sounded exactly like something Aunt Bitty would say. In my mind, I could see her standing in this very room, pointing her finger at Elmer for emphasis, her voice strong with conviction, her emerald eyes flashing.

"And you've already taken care of that?" I asked.

"Yes, although we don't do it here. We take our clients to Dodge City. After the cremation, we bring them back to Winter Break." Elmer stood up and walked over to a door behind him. He disappeared for a few seconds then reentered carrying a small wooden box, which he placed on the desktop in front of me.

With a sick feeling in the pit of my stomach, I realized I was looking at Aunt Bitty's mortal remains. "Th–that's Aunt Bitty?"

His usually insipid smile slipped. "No, Miss Ivy," he said, his voice trembling slightly. "That most certainly is not Bitty Flanagan. You could never reduce a woman like that to a little pile of ash."

As I stared up at him, a tear escaped from the side of his right eye and splashed down on the simple box.

"You got that right, Elmer," Dewey said,

his voice husky.

I felt my own eyes get wet. Strange little Elmer Buskin had cared deeply for Bitty. In that moment, he went from being a parody to a person in my eyes. And I felt true remorse for ever having made fun of him. Aunt Bitty was reaching beyond the grave to teach me one more time that true love includes kindness — and that judging a book by its cover is always a mistake.

"I don't really know much about cremation," I said. "But can't we put Bitty — I mean her remains — into something a little nicer?"

Elmer removed a handkerchief from his pocket. After loudly blowing his nose into it, he sat down again. "This is the container your aunt chose. 'No fuss, Elmer,' she said. 'Don't you let anyone turn my death into more than what it really is. A home-going.' " He shook his head. "Even though it was my intention to respect her wishes, I anticipated your desire to give her a nicer resting place." He pulled open his desk drawer and withdrew a folder. "Here are a few choices for urns. Of course, if you don't see anything here you like, I can order something else." He handed me the pictures, along with his magnifying glass. I could see the pictures just fine without it, but I took it anyway, not wanting to hurt his feelings.

I held the glass over the colorful sheet. There were metal containers as well as some made of stone and wood. There were even some glass urns that looked like something you'd set around the house for decoration. As I was looking over the choices, none of which made me think of Bitty, Elmer reached over and pulled another sheet from underneath the page I was contemplating. He laid it on top of the other glossy advertisements. The flyer displayed a picture of a dark green brass urn in the shape of a book. And on its side was a gold cross. It was just right. It was Bitty. I heard Dewey express his approval.

"Mr. Buskin, this urn is perfect. How long will it take to get it here if I order it immediately?"

Elmer reached down somewhere below his chair. He grunted as he pulled up a cardboard box. After placing it on the table, he opened it and took out the very urn we'd been looking at.

"Now, Elmer," Dewey said. "You already bought it? Must have put you out a pretty penny. What if we hadn't picked it?"

Elmer's eyes twinkled happily. "I just knew this was the one. I felt it in my bones. After awhile, you get some intuition in this business. I picked it up the same day I drove your aunt to Dodge City."

"Thank you, Mr. Buskin," I said gratefully. "You did the right thing. I'll write you a check from Aunt Bitty's account as soon as I get things set up with the bank on Monday morning. How much do I owe you?"

Elmer waved his hand dismissively. "You owe me nothing, Miss Ivy. Your aunt paid good money for everything except this. This is on me. My gift to her."

I started to protest, but Dewey put his hand on my arm and shook his head. In my heart, I understood. Elmer wanted to give something to a woman he respected. I had to let him do it whether he could afford it or not.

"Then I thank you, Mr. Buskin," I said. "And I know that somehow Bitty knows about your kindness, and she appreciates it. If there's anything I can do —"

"Miss Ivy, there *is* something you could do for me," he interrupted. "You could start calling me Elmer instead of Mr. Buskin. It was okay when you were a child, but now you're all grown up. I think friends should be able to call each other by their first names, don't you?"

"I agree. Then you should drop the *Miss*

and just call me Ivy." The words slipped out before I realized I hadn't told him to call me Sam. Great. If I didn't start setting people straight, I was always going to be Ivy Towers to the folks of Winter Break.

We went over the arrangements for a memorial service on Monday afternoon at the church. Elmer told me I could choose to have the urn present during the service or not. It was up to me.

"I don't know," I said carefully. "Why don't you let me think about that. If I decide to display it, what happens after the service?" I was hoping against hope that Bitty hadn't left instructions for her ashes to be scattered somewhere. I saw a sitcom episode once where an intrepid soul, trying to dispose of a relative's remains, hadn't made allowance for wind direction. The ashes were blown back all over him. That scenario gave me the shivers. I didn't want to find myself in a situation that left me trying to wash Aunt Bitty out of my hair.

Elmer cleared his throat. "Well, you can certainly bury the urn in Winter Break Cemetery if you wish, but Bitty didn't intend for that to happen. Your aunt wanted her ashes to stay in the bookstore."

"But how could she possibly request something like that?" I asked. "I have no idea what will happen to the store. What if it doesn't stay a bookstore? What if the new owners don't want to be bothered? What if —"

Dewey stopped me with a touch of his hand, his forehead wrinkled in exasperation. "Ivy Towers. For a smart young woman, sometimes you are rather dense. Haven't you figured it out yet?"

I guess my answer should have been no, because I hadn't a clue what he was talking about. "Figured out what?"

Dewey clucked his tongue and shook his head. "Your aunt left you the bookstore because she hoped you would run it, girl. And she wanted her ashes to stay in the store because as much as she desired to be in the presence of God, she was human. She hoped to leave a little bit of herself in the place she loved the most — with the person she loved the most. You."

I was so taken aback, I could barely speak. "Dewey," I finally sputtered, "I'm in school. I have plans. Why would Bitty think I would give up my life to live in Winter Break?"

Dewey Tater just smiled at me. You know, one of those "you poor little dumb cluck" smiles. Very unchristian thoughts filled my mind. I pushed them away and decided to ignore him.

"Mr. — I mean Elmer, if you would please transfer Bitty to the new urn, I would appreciate it. Let's display it at her funeral. I'll get back to you as to what to do with her . . . uh, remains after the service. Is that okay?"

Elmer nodded while looking back and forth between Dewey and me. I felt like one of two feuding parents trying to decide how to handle custody of their child.

I stood up, shook hands with Elmer, told Dewey I'd see him later, and skedaddled out of the funeral home as fast as I could. My last look at Dewey came as I was going out the front door. He and Elmer Buskin stood in the hallway outside Elmer's office with their arms folded, staring at me as if I were wild game that had just escaped their trap.

I kept my head tugged against my chest to protect my face from freezing while I walked back to the bookstore. I was embarrassed to have acted so strongly to Dewey's declaration of Aunt Bitty's wishes. Why did I feel so defensive? It should be easy for me to tell anyone that life in Winter Break was not my destiny. I had other plans. But it wasn't easy — and I couldn't figure out why.

By the time I got to the bookstore, I was so stiff I had a hard time getting the key in the front door lock. When it finally clicked,

I was close to tears. It wasn't just the outrageous cold; it was everything. My trip to Winter Break had turned into something I hadn't planned on. I was dealing with sadness over Aunt Bitty's death, confusion over my feelings about this small town, and the suspicion that my dear aunt might have actually been murdered.

I slowly peeled off my frozen coat, muffler, and gloves, then danced around a little to get my blood flowing. Good thing I was alone. I'm sure I looked a little loony.

I was almost to the sitting room when I remembered to call Noel Spivey. Those incredible blue eyes floated in front of me. I found myself smiling in spite of myself. I went back to the coatrack and fished his card out of my pocket. I carried it over to Aunt Bitty's desk and sat down. His card read *Noel Spivey — dealer in rare books, specializing in literary first editions, fine printing and binding, artist's books, illustrated books in limited editions, and children's books. Member of ABAA — Antiquarian Booksellers Association of America.* His contact information was at the bottom of the card. It listed a Denver address and phone number. Denver. It seemed so far away from Winter Break, although it wasn't really. Still, I was certain Noel was finding out how different the two places actually were.

I looked up Sarah's number in Bitty's phone book. When she answered, I asked for Noel. He must have been nearby, because it took only a couple of seconds for him to get to the phone. When he said hello, I told him about the service on Monday.

"Thank you, Sam," he said. "I hope you won't think I'm intruding on a difficult time, and I will completely understand if you say no, but I was wondering if we could have dinner together tonight. I promise not to bring up anything about your aunt's books if you'd rather not. It's just that I don't know anyone here, and I'm feeling a little out of my element."

Rather than shouting "Yes, please!" through the receiver and frightening him, I kept my cool and pretended to consider it. However, the idea of heading back to Ruby's made me feel a little dizzy. I quickly formulated a plan and asked him to come to dinner at the bookstore. That way we could eat, and he would get a chance to look around. He happily agreed, and we set a date for seven o'clock. That would give me time to conjure up something a little lighter than Ruby's fare. Besides, I was curious to see what he would offer for Bitty's books. I needed to know all my options.

I put down the phone and found myself staring at the envelope with my name on it, the message begging me to find Bitty's murderer still there, of course. I don't know if a small part of my brain hoped I'd imagined it, but I hadn't. I was still staring at the message and contemplating opening the envelope when the entry bell tinkled and the front door blew open.

Amos stomped inside, trying to knock the ice and snow off his boots and onto the entry rug. I was going to have to get used to the idea that this was actually a public place, and people were going to be walking in whenever they wanted to. Locking the door might help, but during the day, it seemed wrong somehow. Bitty had always welcomed the residents of Winter Break into her cozy bookstore, not only during regular business hours but also at off-hours for group meetings or social get-togethers.

"Hey — Ivy — I mean Sam," he called out.

I was beginning to feel that my name was *Ivy-I-Mean-Sam.* Maybe it would be best to give up and let everyone in Winter Break call me Ivy. I could go back to being Sam when I returned to my other life. Trying to be someone else in Winter Break was close to impossible. It was wearing me out and confusing some of the good people around me.

"Hi, Amos. What's up?" As he hung up his coat, I remembered the envelope in my hand. The drawers of the desk were locked and the keys were in my purse. I carefully slid it under the desk pad while I wondered if I'd ever get a chance to read Bitty's letter.

"I just wanted to know how things were going. Did you get everything squared away with Elmer?"

I started to answer, but Amos didn't wait for a response. He headed straight for the sitting room. Obviously Aunt Bitty hadn't had many conversations in the main store area. The sitting room was like some kind of magnet. People were automatically drawn to it.

I stood up and followed him, hoping he wasn't planning to stay long. I needed to go through Bitty's kitchen to see if I had something to fix for dinner. If not, I'd have to make a trip to Dewey's store. I glanced at the old grandfather clock that sat between two of the floor-to-ceiling bookshelves. I was startled to see it wasn't working. Amos noticed me staring at it and strolled back over to where I stood.

"You actually have to wind it, Ivy — I mean Sam," he said. He took a key off the top of the clock, opened the face, and pulled the weights back up. After setting the correct time, he closed and locked the cabinet and placed the key back where he'd found it.

"I know that, Amos. I used to wind it for Bitty. I just forgot." The steady *ticktock* coming from the clock was a comforting sound. I was surprised I hadn't noticed that it had wound down before now. Its steady tone was an important part of the ambiance of Miss Bitty's Bygone Bookstore. "Amos," I said, "would you do me a favor?"

"Sure, what do you need?" he asked.

"Two things. Would you start a fire in the fireplace? I haven't had time."

"No problem," he said, heading toward the massive stone fireplace. "And the other thing?"

"Stop calling me Sam. It isn't working. I shouldn't have expected people here to see me as anyone but Ivy."

He turned and smiled at me. "It isn't that we can't learn to call you something else; it's just hard to understand the reason behind it. We all know you as Ivy. None of us knows *Sam,* and frankly, I doubt that many people in Winter Break want you to be someone else. We all like Ivy."

I stopped in my tracks and watched him

grab some wood from the wood box. "But what if I am more Sam than Ivy now? Would that disappoint you?"

He positioned the wood in the grate before answering me. When he finished, he turned around once more to stare at me, but this time, he wasn't smiling. "Ivy, I'm sure you've changed some — we all have. I think you see *Sam* as someone more mature and worldly than *Ivy*. But even though we grow up, we still need to accept ourselves as the people God created us to be. I'm not sure you've done that. You can call yourself *Flibber Jibber* for all I care, but maybe it isn't your name you should be thinking about. Maybe you need to find out who the real Ivy Towers is."

I kept my mouth shut, but I could feel the rush of indignation inside me. Amos would never understand the insecurity I'd felt as a teenager. The only place I'd ever felt comfortable with myself was in Winter Break. Out in the real world, I was the kid standing in line, waiting for an invitation to life, trying to find something that would make me feel a part of the world. As Ivy, it had never happened. As Sam, I finally felt I'd made some headway. I wasn't where I wanted to be, but I certainly wasn't where I used to be. I had no intention of going back.

Amos watched me for a few moments, probably waiting for me to acknowledge his advice, but I couldn't think of anything to say that wouldn't start an argument, so I said nothing. Eventually, he went back to building the fire. Out of the corner of my eye, I could see him shaking his head.

Miss Skiffins had come downstairs to see what was going on. She rubbed up against my leg, so I picked her up and brought her into the sitting room. We were getting to be pretty good friends, even though I knew it probably wasn't a good idea. I still didn't have any idea what would happen to her when I left, but I certainly needed to start formulating some kind of plan.

Amos had the fire going but was muttering under his breath.

"Is something wrong, Amos?"

"If you want me to start fires for you, you need to get a set of tongs," he said. "It makes it easier to turn the logs so they'll burn evenly."

He sounded rather cross, and I took exception to it. "Excuse me, but I haven't had much time to go shopping. Perhaps you could look everything over and make me a list of the things I'm lacking. I wouldn't want you to be inconvenienced in any way."

He mumbled something under his breath

that I'm sure wasn't meant to compliment my social skills.

"I don't know why you're getting upset with me, Amos. They're Bitty's tools. Did you lecture her, too?"

He used a poker to flip the logs over. After positioning them the way he wanted them and replacing the fire screen, he sat down in the overstuffed chair next to the hearth. "Bitty Flanagan wouldn't let anyone build a fire in her fireplace, Ivy. She was very independent and liked things a certain way. To tell you the truth, it feels odd to be here without her, using her things."

"I know how to start a fire, you know," I said, still a little annoyed.

"I know you do. Don't get me wrong — I like doing things for people. It makes me feel good. Bitty was a wonderful woman who loved to give to others, but it was hard for her to receive much in return. To tell you the truth, it was a little frustrating."

"I guess it's because she had to spend so much of her life taking care of herself," I said.

"I'm sure that's true," Amos replied. "Sorry I got upset. I guess this whole thing with Bitty has me kinda jumpy."

I smiled at him to let him know he was forgiven. Then I pulled Bitty's rocking chair closer, and Miss Skiffins and I cuddled up in front of the quickly growing fire. As I rocked back and forth, I felt myself begin to relax. I was so comfortable, I could almost forget that the temperature outside was in the single digits. In fact, for a few minutes, I actually forgot that Noel was coming over for dinner and I still hadn't checked out the kitchen for menu possibilities. Remembering the plans I'd made jump-started me out of complacency.

"Amos, I really don't want to rush you, but I have plans tonight, and I still have a lot to do. Did you come over for a reason, or did you just stop by for a visit?"

He was silent for a moment. Finally, he said, "I suppose you're seeing that Spivey guy tonight?"

"How do you know about Noel Spivey?"

"This is Winter Break, Ivy. It doesn't take long for gossip to spread."

I felt my face turn hot. When I was a kid, I'd endured a lot of teasing because my face became a deep crimson when I was angry. It wasn't a good look for me, especially with my dark red hair. I could only hope Amos wouldn't notice. "First of all, it isn't anyone's business who I invite over here," I said. "And second, even though I don't owe you an explanation, Noel is coming over to look at Bitty's books. He's made an offer to buy me out. You should be quite happy about that since you've been trying to get rid of me ever since I got here."

Amos frowned. "Believe me, it isn't that I want you to leave. That's not it at all."

"Amos Parker, there's something you're not telling me. What is it? If it has anything to do with me or Bitty, you need to tell me. I'm not leaving Winter Break until you do."

He sighed and shook his head. "Ivy Towers, you are the most exasperating person I've ever known. The only person more bullheaded than you is . . . me, I guess."

He became quiet and seemed to be turning something over in his mind. His silence amplified the sounds around me: the soft purring that came from the cat that had fallen asleep in my lap, the snapping of the logs in the fireplace, and the steady ticking of the clock behind us.

Finally, he leaned forward in his chair. His fingers were clasped so tightly together, his knuckles were white. The look on his face made my stomach do a flip-flop.

"Ivy," he said slowly, "it is not my intention to frighten you. Believe me, all I want to do is to protect you. But I can see now that the more I push you to leave, the more you're going to dig your heels in."

"You've got that right," I said. "You might as well go on and say what's on your mind."

His hazel eyes locked on mine. "Ivy, it's my belief that Bitty didn't fall off that ladder by accident. I think someone helped her along. And I'm worried that whatever they were after is still here. I want you out of town because I'm afraid your life may be in danger."

5

Amos's pronouncement didn't really surprise me. I was already suspicious about Bitty's death. But hearing someone else say it out loud sent chills running down my spine. And I had to admit that it hadn't occurred to me that I might be at risk. Maybe it was because Bitty's bookstore had always been a safe haven for me, or maybe I hadn't taken the time to think that far ahead. But I was certainly thinking about it now.

I admitted to Amos that I was also suspicious about Bitty's *accident.* "For one thing," I said, "she rode that ladder like it was soldered to her. Then there's the mysterious message I received this morning."

"Message? What message?"

I stood up slowly, trying not to wake Miss Skiffins. I handed her to Amos. "Here, take her. I'll show you."

He took the cat, who opened one sleepy eye to see what was going on then fell right back into contented oblivion.

I went to Bitty's desk and pulled the envelope out from underneath the desk pad where I'd hidden it when Amos arrived. I brought it to him, and as he took it from my hand, I couldn't stop my fingers from trembling. I could only hope he hadn't noticed.

Miss Skiffins was happily cuddled up on the arm of Amos's chair. I decided to leave her where she was. Amos didn't seem to mind having her nearby. Maybe finding Miss Skiffins a good home would be easier than I'd anticipated. I sat down again, waiting for Amos's reaction to the odd note.

"You haven't opened this yet?" he said.

I shook my head. "I will. I . . . I want a few minutes when there aren't any distractions."

"Okay, but don't put it off too long, Ivy. It was important to Bitty that you read it or she wouldn't have left it for you."

"I'm aware of that, Amos." I could feel my temper rising. I pushed it back down. He was only trying to help.

"Do you have any idea who wrote this?" he asked after rereading the message carefully.

"None. The envelope was on the desk where I left it before I took a shower.

Someone wrote that while I was upstairs."

"Was the front door locked?"

I shrugged. "I've gone over and over it in my mind, Amos. The last person here before I went upstairs was Dewey Tater. I walked him to the door, but I can't remember whether or not I locked it. I thought I did. Dewey had just given me Bitty's keys. It would have made sense for me to use them. I had it in my mind to lock the door because I didn't want anyone wandering in while I was in the shower. The problem is, I don't actually remember turning the lock." I shook my head. "I'm sorry. I just can't say for certain."

"It's okay," Amos said. "Who else has keys to this place, Ivy?"

"As far as I know, I'm the only one. It's possible Dewey might have another set. Maybe Isaac, but I'm not certain about that."

"Isaac Holsapple? When was the last time you saw him?"

"I haven't seen him at all. He hasn't been around."

"I suppose that's not unusual," Amos said. "He only worked for Bitty the first half of the week. Isaac came in on Mondays to start cataloging the new books. Tuesdays, he put the cataloged books on the shelves, and

Wednesdays, he went to the post office to bring over any new shipments. Sometimes your aunt would let him open the new boxes, but that was it. She did everything else."

"What about the rest of the week?"

"On Thursdays, Bitty sorted through all the new books that had come in and prepared any books that were supposed to be mailed out. She took those books to the post office on Friday. She wouldn't let anyone else mail out books. She'd hand them personally to Alma because she wanted to make certain they were processed immediately."

This was understandable. Everyone knew that Alma Pettibone had a tendency to get caught up in her daytime soaps, and sometimes letters and packages didn't get prepared in time for the regular pickup. If you had something important to mail, it was best to stand at the counter and watch while Alma stamped it and put it in the pickup bin.

I was surprised. "You certainly know a lot about the goings-on in the bookstore."

He shrugged. "Bitty and I were friends, Ivy. I tried to stop by every day. You didn't have to spend much time with Bitty to figure out her schedule. She was as regular as . . . well, that old grandfather clock — once you wind it, that is."

I ignored the dig at my failure to attend to Bitty's clock. "You said Isaac found her Wednesday morning?"

"Yes. He went to the post office around ten. After he brought the mail back, Bitty sent him to Dewey's for some packaging tape, and then to Ruby's to pick up a couple of egg salad sandwiches. I guess they always ate egg salad together on Wednesdays. It was their habit."

"What time did he find Bitty?"

"He picked up the sandwiches a little after eleven. He called me about eleven thirty."

"Are you the only one he called?"

"No," Amos said. "Before he called me, he called Lucy. I mean Dr. Barber."

Amos looked a little uncomfortable when he mentioned the new doctor. I wondered why. "I thought Dr. Barber's office was in Hugoton."

"You're right; it is. But she was in town that morning, checking on Huey Martin's lumbago. Isaac saw her when he was at Ruby's. He called her over there."

I thought about the timeline. "So Isaac leaves Ruby's a little after eleven. It only takes a few minutes to walk here from Ruby's, yet it takes him over twenty minutes to call you? Does that seem reasonable?"

Amos absently ran his hands through his hair, a familiar sign of frustration. "I don't know, Ivy. I asked Lucy what time he called her. She couldn't quite remember. After she got here and realized that Bitty was beyond help, she told Isaac to call me." He stared past me, his forehead wrinkled in thought. "There wasn't much time for him to do anything except what he says he did. Besides," he said, "Isaac worshipped your aunt. I don't believe for one minute he would ever do anything to hurt her."

I wasn't as confident as Amos. I'd always thought Isaac was a little strange. Although he mostly kept to himself, he used to make me feel distinctly uncomfortable. I asked Bitty about him once. She'd looked at me sternly and said, "Now, Ivy, God made everyone different. Just because someone isn't just like you, it doesn't mean that He hasn't stuffed that person full of beautiful gifts."

Maybe so, but I'd never been able to find anything remotely beautiful about Isaac Holsapple. He was small and hunched over with a big nose and squinty eyes. His long salt-and-pepper hair was always messy, even though his clothes were always perfectly ironed and in place. He'd moved to Winter

Break and started working for Bitty many years ago, not long after she opened the bookstore. Her fiancé, Robert, had been killed in an accident. Mother told me that Bitty had thrown herself into the bookstore so she could "forget." When I was a young girl, the story made me sad. But I'd never seen my great-aunt spend one moment sorrowing over what might have been. She was too busy enjoying life, the people around her, and the bookstore she loved.

"You haven't told me why you're suspicious about Bitty's death," I said.

Amos leaned back in his chair. "There are several things that bother me, Ivy. As you said, Bitty was an expert on that ladder. She was in good shape for her age. In fact, she was in better shape than most people half her age." He stared at the crackling flames in the fireplace. "Then there's the position of her body. It just didn't look quite right to me."

I didn't like the images that came into my mind as I imagined Bitty falling from her trusty library ladder, so I decided to push on. "Anything else, Amos?"

He nodded. "You may think this is silly, but there is something else that worries me."

"At this point, everything is important. Tell me."

He rubbed his hands together as though he were cold even though we sat in front of a roaring fire. I understood how he felt. The idea of anyone harming Aunt Bitty made me feel that I'd been dropped outside in a snowbank. It not only didn't make sense; it was unfathomable.

"Your aunt was the most organized person I ever knew," Amos said. "Her life ran like a well-oiled machine. She had a plan for everything, and she worked that plan as if it were cut in stone and delivered by the Lord God Himself.

"Every morning she and Dewey Tater had breakfast at 7:00 a.m. I know this because I used to stop by and eat with them whenever I could. At eight thirty, Dewey left to open his store, and Bitty cleaned up the breakfast dishes. She put those dishes in the dishwasher, turned it on, and started getting ready to open the bookstore at precisely nine o'clock. I watched her follow this same pattern every morning I was here. It never changed unless it was a day when she had to go to Hugoton for a doctor's or dentist's appointment, or if she drove out of town for an auction or estate sale."

"I know Aunt Bitty was organized to the max, but what does that have to do with anything?"

"I'm getting there," he said, looking a little perturbed by my interruption. "Sometimes during the day, she might fix herself a cup of herbal tea, but that was usually only in the afternoon."

I interrupted him. "Amos, I still don't see why this is important."

He lowered his voice as if someone else could hear us, but unless Miss Skiffins planned to sell our secrets for catnip, we were pretty safe. "I told you this might sound like an odd thing to be concerned about, but the morning Bitty died, there were two cups with saucers sitting on the kitchen cabinet."

"Oh, Amos. That doesn't sound like an important clue. Maybe she was making tea for her and Isaac."

"No way. Isaac doesn't drink anything with caffeine in it. Says it makes him too nervous. I've known him a long time. He's almost religious about it."

"Okay. What if Bitty didn't have time to run the dishwasher?" I offered.

He shook his head again. "The dishwasher had been turned on that morning. I checked it. The dishes inside it were warm. Besides a few other dishes, probably from the previous night's dinner, there were two cups and two small plates from breakfast. And anyway, these weren't empty cups, Ivy. There were tea bags still sitting inside them and a pan of water heating on the stove. By the time I found it, the water was almost all boiled away."

"So you think someone was here Wednesday morning."

"Yes. Bitty was making tea because she was expecting company. The problem is, I've asked everyone I can think of, and no one admits to stopping by."

I thought for a moment. "Could it have been a book buyer from out of town?"

"No. No one saw any cars out front Wednesday morning. As nosy as everyone is in this town, someone would have noticed a strange car."

"So you believe that between the time Isaac left and the time he came back, someone came into the bookstore without being seen by anyone else in town and killed Aunt Bitty."

Amos held up his hands in mock surrender. "I know it sounds unlikely, but I just can't shake the feeling that something besides a simple accident happened here. And now with this . . ." He held up the envelope with the scrawled note.

"Amos, if you thought Bitty's death looked suspicious, why didn't you call someone?

Start an investigation? And why let Elmer take her body before an expert had a chance to look at her injuries?"

He sighed. "Because this is Winter Break, Ivy. No one gets murdered here. Dr. Barber called it an accident. I figured she'd know. And to be honest, I was so upset about losing Bitty, I didn't start putting all of this together until after she had already been sent to Dodge City. By that time, it was too late. And before you ask, I can't call anyone from the outside in now to investigate. I don't have a shred of evidence except a couple of teacups. Believe me, I get the Andy Taylor treatment enough without having to go out of my way to stir it up."

The grandfather clock in the bookstore bonged a warning that my time was running out. "Look," I said, standing up, "you've got to get out of here so I can get ready for my meeting with Noel Spivey. We'll talk more about this tomorrow after church, okay?"

Amos reached over and patted Miss Skiffins once more before pulling himself up from his chair. "Okay. But hide that envelope. Lock it up. If the person who killed Bitty is still in town, the last thing we want to do is to tip anyone off that we're suspicious."

I'd already started toward the front door, when Amos grabbed my arm and spun me around. "Listen, Ivy. I still think you should leave town. The only reason anyone would have to murder your aunt was because she had something someone wanted. We don't know if it's still here or not. If it is . . ."

As I gazed into his eyes, I felt a stirring of something I thought was buried long ago. The last thing I wanted was to have feelings for Amos Parker. After all, those emotions belonged to Ivy, not to me. I pulled away from him.

"First of all, Amos, if there was something in here that someone wanted badly enough to kill for it, it's long gone by now. I mean, think about it. This place has been basically unprotected since Bitty died. I don't believe you need to worry about that any longer."

He shrugged. "You could be right. But if the killer finds out you're snooping around, trying to find out what really happened, you could be putting yourself in danger."

"You listen to me, Amos Parker. If someone really did kill my aunt Bitty, there's no way I'm leaving Winter Break until we catch him. You and I have to put our heads together and solve this. Bitty deserves no less."

Amos walked over to the door and pulled

his coat from the rack. "You're right. But I want you to be careful. You have to start locking this door. Don't open it unless you're sure it's safe. And don't tell anyone about our suspicions." He zipped up his coat and pointed his finger at me. "And I mean *anyone.* Not even Dewey. Okay?"

"Too late," I said sheepishly. "I already mentioned something to Dewey."

Amos's forehead wrinkled with concern. "What did he say?"

"He got really upset, Amos. He wouldn't even discuss it."

"Can't say I'm surprised. He's been through a lot. Dewey loved your aunt very much. He was really hurt when she postponed their wedding."

His words took me by surprise. "What? I . . . I didn't know that. Do you know why?"

Amos shrugged. "I have no idea. Whatever it was, it didn't seem to change their relationship much. They still spent every day together." He pulled on his hat. "You remember what I said. Be careful, okay?"

"I will. I promise."

As he turned to walk out the door, I called out to him. "Andy Taylor was a better lawman than any of those big-city detectives who looked down on him, you know. And he was always right."

Amos's slow smile told me that he understood. I watched him leave and was surprised to find myself missing him.

6

By the time Amos left, I had only a couple of hours to get ready for Noel Spivey's visit. A quick trip upstairs told me that Dewey had given me enough supplies to put together a dinner for two. It wouldn't be fancy, but it would be food.

I got dressed, tried to do something with my hair, and applied a little makeup. Then I threw together a tuna casserole and popped it in the oven. Thankfully, Dewey had put a package of rolls in the bread box. A can of corn rounded out the meal. I poured the corn into a pan and turned the burner on low. After adding a little butter and salt, I cast a critical eye at Bitty's kitchen. Although it was certainly cozy, it was really too small for company. I decided to serve dinner on the big table in the sitting room.

After carrying our place settings and silverware downstairs, I remembered that I'd promised my mother a phone call.

"Shoot," I said out loud. Miss Skiffins looked up from the chair where Amos had left her. She gazed at me wide-eyed, as if disturbing her sleep was a punishable offense in her world. "Sorry," I said softly. She made a little trilling noise, signaling absolution, I guess. Then she closed her eyes once again.

I ran upstairs, trying to remember the time difference between the United States and China. Mother had told me more than once. What was it? Were they thirteen or fourteen hours ahead of us or behind us? Either my parents were still in bed or they'd been up only a short time. I decided to call them after dinner. I was pretty sure they'd be happier to hear from me when they were fully awake. What was that proverb about greeting someone early in the morning? I couldn't quite remember it word for word, but I was pretty sure the writer wasn't encouraging the practice. Besides, it was never a good idea to talk to my mother before she had her first cup of coffee. Mother had very few vices, but coffee was something she enjoyed with a vengeance. I had to hope she could get some in China; otherwise some of her conversions were going to be taken by force.

After setting the table, I brought the tuna

casserole down last. I didn't like the way Miss Skiffins was eyeing it, so I made one last trek upstairs to lock her up. She would have to go in Bitty's bedroom since my room didn't have a door. Funny how I'd been here almost twenty-four hours and still hadn't ventured into my aunt's room.

I slowly turned the door handle. Miss Skiffins looked up into my face as if asking if she was finally going to see her beloved mistress. I'm sure she was wondering why she'd been stuck with me instead of her rightful owner. As I opened the door, the aroma of my aunt's perfume was like a gentle caress. *Jean Nate.* It was the only fragrance she wore. I sucked in a deep breath, trying to ignore the lump in my throat.

While I fumbled for the light switch, Miss Skiffins wriggled out of my arms. She ran straight for the bed and jumped up on the colorful quilted comforter. I entered the room, closing the door behind me so she couldn't escape. After sniffing around a little, probably looking for Bitty, she conceded defeat and curled up next to the pillows.

I didn't have much time, but I spent the next few moments breathing in Bitty's presence. It was almost as if she were still here.

Her lilac housecoat with its pale ivory ribbons lay on an old Victorian-styled chair in the corner that had belonged to her mother. Various framed pictures adorned the walls and dresser. A closer look revealed that the childish drawings were mine, and most of the photographs were of me. It had been years since I'd visited this room. Even when I'd stayed here, I'd kept to my own room, not thinking that an old woman's bedroom would hold anything of interest to me.

It was evident that Bitty had seen me almost as her own child. And perhaps in some ways it was true. In many aspects she had been more of a mother to me than my own had. I felt a deep stab of grief. Not for Bitty; I knew where she was, and I knew she was happy. It was the idea that there would be no more Bitty Flanagan in the world. I felt that we had all lost something important. Something that couldn't be replaced. I was certain I would never again find anyone quite like her.

Miss Skiffins was already fast asleep, probably dreaming of Bitty. I quietly closed the door and went downstairs to wait for Noel.

He knocked on the door at precisely seven o'clock. As he stepped inside, I was struck once again by how gorgeous he was. I didn't want to be too impressed; I knew that what was inside a person was more important than the outside, but I could certainly appreciate the excellent job God had done on the exterior of this man. It would be downright disrespectful to ignore His fine handiwork.

He took off his coat and hung it on the coatrack, taking special care to make sure it was secure. He wore designer jeans and a cerulean blue cable-knit sweater that complemented his azure eyes and dark hair.

"Thank you for asking me over, Sam," he said, smiling. "I know this is a difficult time for you."

"It's okay. I have been a little worried about what to do with the bookstore. You might be an answer to prayer. But let's eat first. Then we'll talk business, okay?"

He nodded his agreement, flashing me another one of his million-dollar smiles.

I'd felt pretty good about how I looked until that moment. Being honest with myself, I had to accept the unfortunate truth that I wasn't the prettiest person in the room anymore.

As I showed him to the sitting room, he stopped near a display case that held some special books Bitty kept under lock and key. Even in the low light of the store, I saw his face pale. "Oh my goodness," he said softly.

"Do you know what these are?"

I circled back to where he stood, gazing into the glass-covered case. "Yes. My aunt told me those were all first editions of C. S. Lewis's Chronicles of Narnia series. Some of them are signed by the illustrator, Pauline . . . something."

"Baynes. Pauline Baynes. Are you certain? Do you know which ones are signed?"

I shook my head. "Although I don't know much about any of the other books here, Aunt Bitty spoke to me about this set more than once. She was quite proud of it. As you can see, she had collected only four of the set. There are seven, I believe. If I remember right, two of these books are signed and two are not."

I swear, if he hadn't been a rather refined person, I think he would have drooled on the glass.

"Are they worth much?" I asked.

The look he gave me made me realize that I didn't have enough knowledge about Bitty's books to sell them. I was going to have to sharpen my rare book smarts.

"Sam, I would have to inspect them to give you an accurate estimate, but you're looking at somewhere around ten to twelve thousand dollars here. And if *The Silver Chair* is one of the books signed by

Baynes . . . well, a book like that just sold for nine thousand dollars."

Now it was my turn to feel the blood drain from my face. "Goodness gracious," I said. "I . . . I had no idea."

He frowned. "Making you an offer on your stock is going to be difficult if you don't know the value of it."

I felt really stupid. Why in the world did Bitty leave me this bookstore? She had to know I was ignorant about it. Then I remembered what Dewey told me at the funeral home. Bitty expected me to stay here and run things. I guess she thought I'd learn as I went. Now I was in a pickle.

"Look, let's eat. Then we'll talk about the store. To be honest, I haven't decided whether I'm going to sell it or keep it."

Noel seemed to take my declaration calmly and proceeded over to the table for dinner. I, on the other hand, couldn't believe what I'd just said. I had no intention of keeping the bookstore. Where in the world had those words come from?

Noel was busy looking at our dinner fare, so I risked a look up at the ceiling while I reminded my aunt that I had a life and she needed to quit interfering in it.

"Everything looks good," Noel said, breaking me out of my one-way discussion with

Aunt Bitty.

I wondered if he was being kind. It occurred to me that he was probably used to high-class fare. A simple tuna casserole might be too pedestrian for his tastes. I stood there in my simple denim smock and twenty-dollar department store faux-suede Mary Janes, feeling out of place and ignorant. I was fourteen again — a goofy, gawky nerd. I had to remind myself that the insecure little girl was gone. I was Sam: smart, savvy, and mature. Why had I suddenly dropped back into the role of the teenager who never felt she belonged?

"It . . . it might not be what you're used to," I said, hoping I didn't sound as unsure as I felt.

I was rewarded with another utterly disarming smile. "I'm on the road so much, I'm used to greasy fast-food hamburgers and cold, stringy chicken. This is a banquet." He pulled out a chair for me. "I'm so hungry, I'm liable to forget my manners and dig in before you have a chance to get to the table. For your own good, I think you'd better sit down."

I obeyed, and within a few seconds we were eating. The casserole was good. I'd made it the way Aunt Bitty had taught me. In fact, most of my cooking expertise came from Bitty. Mother wasn't a very good cook. Preparing meals had always been a chore for her. Aunt Bitty had loved to cook, and she had always taken the time to teach me her recipes. She even allowed me to make dinner from time to time. Pretty heady stuff to a teenager.

Noel really did seem to be enjoying his meal, and I found myself relaxing a little. "So you deal in rare books," I said between bites. "Do you have a store?"

He shook his head. "No, almost all my work is done on the Internet and through private bidders."

I smiled. "Aunt Bitty never took to the Internet. She said she liked to deal with human beings face-to-face, not through a computer screen."

Noel laughed. "That sounds like Bitty. I talked to her more than once about setting up an Internet store, but she wasn't interested. Your aunt was very independent."

"You're right about that, but I think she did pretty well for herself. I'm amazed by what I've found since I got here. I never realized my aunt was so knowledgeable."

Noel reached for another roll. "She knew a lot about books, Sam, but she didn't know much about business. She could have made five times the money if she'd put her business on the Net. She built up customers slowly and carefully over time, but the Internet brings in thousands of customers who are looking for exactly what you have. The idea of a bookstore in a small town like this . . . Well, it just isn't practical."

I watched him slather butter on his roll. For some reason I felt defensive, and I couldn't understand why. What he said made sense. Why did I want to jump up and demand that he take it back? After swallowing the bitter bile of resentment that filled my throat, I said timidly, "But I love this bookstore." He looked at me with pity. Not quite what I was going for.

"I know. I'm sorry. This store means something to you because it belonged to your aunt. I was talking strictly from a business viewpoint. I should have been more understanding."

My temporary flash of temper melted away. After all, he was so cute. . . .

"Let's talk about you for a while, Sam," he said. "Tell me about your life. What do you do when you're not in Winter Break?"

I told him about school, tried to explain my parents, which wasn't easy, and talked about graduation and my general lack of direction. By the time I quit jabbering, he was finished eating. My plate was still full,

111

but I really wasn't hungry anyway. It was nice to have someone ask about my life as if he were really interested.

I wolfed down a few bites, just enough to make it look as if I'd given it the old college try. When I pushed my plate away, Noel poured us both some coffee from the carafe I'd filled and placed on the table so I wouldn't have to go back upstairs. He was quiet as he filled our cups, and his face was knit in a frown. Finally, he said, "Sam, I think you're a very smart, capable woman. I'm going to make you a very nice offer for the inventory in this bookstore. I'm also going to suggest something to you. You don't have to answer now, but I would like you to think about it." He sipped his coffee and stared at me for a moment before continuing. "I think you should take the money I give you and come to Denver. You'll have enough money for a nice apartment and a sufficient income to live on for a while. I have a friend who runs a large publishing house just outside the city. He's just expanded and is looking for additional staff. You'd be a cinch for the job of acquisitions editor. It pays great and you'd be able to work with books and authors. You'd love it."

"It sounds wonderful, Noel, but I haven't

graduated yet. I won't get my degree until the spring."

He leaned across the table and took my hand. "Don't worry about that. If I recommend you, you'll get the job. Finish your degree later if you want to."

The confusion over what to do with my life lifted. Here was a chance to use my knowledge about literature in a way that would be fun and exciting. My mouth was ready to shout "Yes!" but for some reason, "Let me think about it" came out instead.

He squeezed my hand. "Of course. I completely understand. You don't know me very well, and this is all very sudden." He gazed into my eyes while my heart did flip-flops like a frantic little fish out of water. "I'd really like us to get to know each other, Sam. I think you're a very special person. I intend to hang around for a few days after the funeral, if it's okay."

"It's definitely okay," I said impulsively.

He pressed my hand again and grinned. "Great."

I stared dumbly at him until I realized it was my turn to talk. "Let me get these dishes," I said. "Would you like some ice cream? All I have is butter pecan." Amos had obviously had a hand in that selection. He knew butter pecan was my very favorite ice cream. When looking for dinner pos-sibilities, I'd found a half gallon of it in the freezer.

"Sounds great," Noel said. "Can I help with the dishes?"

Under normal circumstances, I might have accepted his offer, but I needed some time to myself, so I declined. I wanted to check my hair and makeup and try to lower my heart rate a little. Passing out in front of Noel Spivey wasn't something I wanted to do. Having "the vapors" was passé, and it was way too early in our relationship for mouth-to-mouth resuscitation — although the idea was definitely interesting.

I gathered our dishes together and headed upstairs. I could feel his eyes on me, and it made me nervous. The plates rattled slightly in my trembling hands. I hoped he didn't realize how much he affected me. I didn't want to come off as some naive country bumpkin. Instead, I wanted to appear to be the kind of woman who could be an acquisi-tions editor, although I wasn't sure what one looked like. To be honest, I wasn't even certain what an acquisitions editor did. But at the moment, I didn't really care. Noel would be in Denver. I would be in Denver. That was really all that mattered.

I made it to the kitchen and put the plates

on the counter. Then I searched for a couple of bowls. I'd just pulled the ice cream out of the freezer when I remembered seeing some caramel syrup when I was going through the cabinets. Sure enough, I found a jar sitting next to the sugar. I loved it slopped all over my ice cream and wondered if Noel might like some, too. I could have just taken it downstairs and let Noel decide if he wanted some, but I was afraid to carry too much at one time. Falling on my fanny in front of the man I might marry someday wouldn't get us started out on the right foot.

I started back down the stairs but stopped before I had a chance to call out to Noel. He was squatting next to Bitty's desk, going through the boxes of books that had come in before she died. He seemed frantic and upset. At one point, I heard him use a word that had probably never been uttered before in Miss Bitty's Bygone Bookstore.

I watched him for several seconds, unsure of what to do. Finally, I crept backward up the stairs so he wouldn't see or hear me. Then I went back to the kitchen, spooned out the ice cream, and returned to the stairs. I clomped down each step like some kind of loopy elephant, wanting to make certain he heard me. Fortunately, he was no longer near the boxes as I ventured downstairs. As

I turned the corner at the bottom, I saw that he was back at the table in the sitting room, looking as if he'd been there the whole time.

I was confused. What was he looking for? If he wanted to know what was in those boxes, why hadn't he just asked me? I tried to reassure myself that he was probably looking out after his own interests. If he was going to buy my books, he wanted to know what he was getting. But I still couldn't understand why he hadn't waited. I gladly would have shown him everything.

"Here you go," I said, setting a bowl in front of him. "Sorry I took so long."

He gave me that Cary Grant smile of his. Or Hugh Grant, for people who don't love old movies the way I do. "No problem. I enjoy sitting here. It's a lovely room."

"Thank you. When Aunt Bitty bought this house, she transformed it into what it is now. I think she did a wonderful job of keeping its Victorian charm. Almost everything is original except for the paint, wallpaper, and of course, the bookshelves."

"Really. How interesting." He picked up his spoon and started in on his ice cream.

We talked very little while we ate. I liked Noel very much. He was handsome, successful, handsome, charming, handsome . . .

Okay, I clearly needed to reset my priorities, but goodness gracious, he was so hand— never mind.

I'd planned to let him look through the books after dinner, but now I wasn't comfortable with it. Aunt Bitty used to tell me that if something felt wrong, God was probably giving you a warning. It was best to pay attention. I decided to go with her advice.

I took one last bite and pushed the bowl away. "Noel," I said, "I'm terribly sorry, but I'd like to wait until after the service on Monday to go through the inventory. I hope you don't mind, but I'm awfully tired. Are you upset?"

"Of course not," he said with sincerity. "I already told you that we didn't need to do this now. Let's leave it alone until Tuesday, shall we?"

"Thank you. I appreciate your understanding." I gave him my best smile, the one Aunt Bitty used to call my "try guessing what I'm up to" smirk. I hoped Noel wouldn't interpret it the same way.

He stood up. "Thank you for the wonderful dinner. It was such a nice break from restaurant food." He shook his head. "I had lunch at the restaurant down the street today. The food was quite good, but the owner was a little . . . I don't know. Worrisome, I guess."

Even though I had other things on my mind, I had to laugh. "Yes, Ruby is certainly different, but she's okay."

His expression told me he wasn't convinced. I was so used to the eccentricities of the citizens of Winter Break that I'd forgotten how they must appear to normal people.

As I walked him to the door, I noticed that his gaze swung toward the boxes in the corner. I'd already decided to go through those boxes after he left. I wanted to know exactly what was in them.

After putting on his coat, Noel turned to me. "Thank you, Sam, for allowing me to spend time with you. I truly enjoyed myself. I wish we'd met under different circumstances."

Before I had a chance to brace myself, he bent down and kissed me on the cheek. His lips were soft, and he smelled like expensive aftershave lotion and leather. It wasn't an unpleasant combination.

After he left, I went to the desk and got the key. I was careful to lock the door. Peeping through a window shade that covered one of the front windows, I watched him get in his car and drive away.

A line from *Alice in Wonderland* and

Through the Looking Glass by Lewis Carroll flashed through my mind.

"Curiouser and curiouser," I said softly to myself.

7

I washed the dishes and cleaned up the table in the sitting room. The whole time my mind kept turning over the suspicions Amos had about Bitty's death. His comments had only created more questions. Why would anyone want to kill Bitty? Who was she expecting the morning she died? And who wrote that message on the envelope?

I was also bothered by the fact that my aunt broke off her engagement with Dewey. Why? Did she find out something about him that concerned her? Could he have hurt her because of it? I had to admit that Dewey Tater was the last person I would suspect of murder, but at this point, I couldn't afford to rule anyone out.

And what about Isaac Holsapple? He'd always seemed absolutely devoted to Bitty. Yet it was odd that he still hadn't shown his face, especially since he lived in the apartment next door. During her original renovations, Bitty had sectioned off part of the house and turned it into small, separate living quarters. I had no idea why; perhaps she knew she'd need an assistant someday and wanted to be ready. Isaac moved in a few months after the bookstore opened.

According to Amos, Isaac was the one who found Bitty's body. Maybe he'd killed her then covered it up by calling the doctor and Amos. But why? Could there be something in the bookstore he wanted? Something valuable? That possibility seemed unlikely. If Isaac had his eye on something, why didn't he just take it and leave town? In all these years, there must have been a number of valuable books. Why kill her now?

I had to set some time aside to carefully inspect Bitty's accounting books. If there was anything unusual, chances were I would find it there. Tonight I'd look through her new shipment. I wished I could ask Noel for help. As an expert, he could certainly tell me if there was anything valuable among the old books. But how could I trust him? After catching him going through those boxes, I had to wonder if he had some kind of ulterior motive. Besides, if he wanted to make an offer on the inventory, what would prevent him from lying about the value of

Bitty's stock? It was hard to distrust him. I really liked him, and my gut told me he was a good person. But my gut had also told me that wrapping up Bitty's affairs in Winter Break wouldn't take much effort. That's why it's not a good idea to always go with your gut, no matter what the detective novels say. Not that I would know anything about that, of course.

I had to find a way to learn a lot about rare and collectible books, and I needed to do it yesterday. The Internet would be a great source of information, but Aunt Bitty didn't have a computer. I didn't want to mess with setting up service in the bookstore since I didn't plan to be in Winter Break very long. I remembered seeing a computer on Elmer's desk. I wondered if he'd either let me use it or allow me to connect my laptop up there. I decided to ask him tomorrow at church.

In the meantime, Amos and I would have to poke around to see if we could catch a murderer. There was always the possibility that Bitty's killer was someone I didn't know. If that was the case, uncovering the truth was going to be very difficult.

I finished the dishes, released Miss Skiffins from her temporary prison, and went downstairs to look through the books Noel had found so interesting. I also intended to read Bitty's letter. For some reason I dreaded it. Not because I didn't love her to pieces, but because I felt guilty about not visiting her for so long. I was afraid her letter would make me feel even worse than I did now, if that was possible.

I checked the time. It was a little after nine. Mother and Dad would definitely be up and around by now. I'd written their number down on a piece of paper and put it in my pocket. I pulled it out and sat down at Bitty's desk. I dialed all the numbers, but I kept getting a message telling me that the circuits were busy. Finally, I dialed 00 for the international operator. About a minute later, the phone was ringing at the mission. I heard someone pick up the receiver.

"*Wei. Ni hao?*"

Per my mother's instructions, I responded with "*Qing jiao* Mr. and Mrs. Towers?"

"Ivy, is that you?" my father said.

"Dad?"

"Yes, dear. Who else did you think it would be?"

"I didn't recognize your voice. You sound like a native."

"Of course it's me. However, your mother did meet a very handsome Chinese gentleman last night who seemed quite taken with

123

her. If you call again and another man answers the phone, you'll know I've been summarily dismissed."

"Now, Dad. You know Mother couldn't do without you."

"Let's hope so. She's been giving me the fish eye all morning. I may be on my way out."

In the background, I heard my mother say, "Oh, Mickey. Sometimes you are so ridiculous! Give me that phone."

"I have to go, sweetie. Here's Mother."

I barely had time to say good-bye before my mother's voice came through the receiver. "Ivy. How are you? Are you in Winter Break?"

I proceeded to tell her where I was and what was going on. Well, not everything. I had no intention of sharing my suspicions about Bitty's death. Mother wasn't the type to believe in conspiracies or evil agendas. If I told her the truth, she would have considered me completely batty and insisted that I go home. In my mother's eyes, I was still twelve years old, slightly fumble brained, and wandering through life in some kind of hopeless fog.

"Now, Ivy, you will have everything wrapped up before school starts, won't you?" she asked after my recitation.

"That's my plan, Mother."

"School is the most important thing. Even with only an English degree, you'll be ahead of some job seekers who have no degree at all."

The little jab about my degree made it all the way through the electronic signals that connected Winter Break to Beijing. Funny how being thousands of miles away from my parents still didn't offer any protection from my mother's disapproval.

I'd like to think that what I said next was completely unplanned. In a way it was, and in another way, it wasn't. Suffice it to say that as soon as the words were out of my mouth, I wanted to push them back down my throat. But there it was. . . . "Mother, the funniest thing. Dewey Tater says that Aunt Bitty wanted me to stay in Winter Break and run the bookstore. What do you think of that?"

The number of miles separating us made absolutely no difference. My mother's reaction covered the distance in record time. I was surprised there wasn't a sonic boom.

"Ivy Samantha Towers! That's the most ridiculous thing I ever heard," she sputtered. "How could you possibly consider an idea like that? It's bad enough that Aunt Bitty threw her life away to live in that one-horse town, but to think that my own daughter would ever consider doing the same thing? Why, it's . . . it's . . . it's ludicrous. That's what it is. Ludicrous!"

Putting her out of her misery was the only kind thing to do. "Relax, Mother. I didn't say I seriously considered it. I know I have to go back and finish my last semester. Don't worry."

Mother gave an audible sigh of relief. "Well, thank goodness for small favors. I'm glad you're being sensible about this." She was silent for a moment. "Look, Ivy. I know you loved your aunt. I did, too. She was my mother's sister. But we have to remind ourselves that God has a plan for our lives. In my opinion, Bitty's independent spirit led her on the wrong path. She never found her purpose. I don't want the same for you. Remember that Daddy and I would love to have you come here after graduation. You're smart when it comes to language. You could pick up Mandarin in no time at all, and you could be so much help to us. You keep that in mind, okay?"

"Yes, Mother. I will."

I said good-bye to both of them, promising to call again in a few days. When I put the phone down, my emotions were all jumbled up. I really did want to find God's will for my life. Anyway, I thought I did. Maybe I was waiting for a bush to burn. It would probably take something just as dramatic, because so far, I wasn't picking up anything that remotely resembled a road map for my future. I tried to push my mother's voice out of my head. It was getting late, and I still had things to do.

I sat down on the floor next to the two new boxes of books. I went through the first box. Seventeen books. All old. All in pretty good shape. Most were first editions. At least I knew enough to look for that. There were some books by Mark Twain, as well as some from Zane Grey. There were several books by authors I'd never heard of, a couple of books of poetry, and a first edition of *The Pilgrim's Progress and Other Allegorical Works* by John Bunyan. Of course, I had no idea of their value. It would be fun to research them, though.

I finally finished the first box. I left the books stacked up on the floor, next to their respective box. I wanted to make a list of titles and authors for my investigation. Then I moved to the second box. Inside were books containing art by Norman Rockwell, several children's books, a set of Dickenses without a printing date, and once again, several other books by authors I didn't recognize.

At the bottom of the second box, I found a note that would have been impossible to see unless the books were removed.

Dear Miss Flanagan,

As I packed up these boxes, I discovered a few additional books. They may not have any value. If they do, you can just send me whatever you think is fair. This is a very difficult time. Thank you for being so understanding and compassionate. Your honesty and concern have made things easier.

The note was signed *Olivia.*

I had no idea who Olivia was. Neither did I know what Noel was looking for in these boxes. I decided to put his unusual behavior in my mental file titled "Things That Seem Suspicious." That file was getting remarkably full.

I pushed myself up from the floor and unlocked the desk drawer. Then I removed the envelope with Bitty's letter and sat down to read it. A blast of cold air from the front windows made me decide that I would rather sit in front of the fire. Although the bookstore itself was fairly warm, the icy temperatures outside made the area near the front of the store much colder than anywhere else in the old building.

I pulled up one of the shades to see big, fat flakes of snow falling lazily from the sky. The streetlight outside highlighted their leisurely dance. I watched for a few minutes, taking in their incredible beauty. Funny how Wichita hardly ever saw snow anymore, while Winter Break seemed to draw it like a magnet. I'd really missed it.

I'd started to think a lot about Christmas. My original plan had been to go back to school and stay in one of the dorm rooms rented to students who had nowhere else to go during the break. However, the way things were going, it was beginning to look as if I might need to stay in town awhile longer. Of course, that would mean Christmas in Winter Break.

Bitty and I had enjoyed quite a few holidays together, but Christmas was my favorite. She had made everything so special. Evenings spent by the fire, reading various Christmas stories and drinking hot chocolate; decorating the bookstore together; sitting next to her while she read the story of the birth of Christ from the Bible; standing outside and gazing up at the stars on Christmas Eve, thanking the Lord for His amazing love. All these memories came pouring back into my mind. I'd forgotten about them, relegating them to that invisible closet into which I'd shoved almost all of my Winter Break memories.

A little *meow* and the feel of soft cat hair on my leg reminded me that I also had to look after Miss Skiffins until I could find her a new home. I'd meant to talk to Amos about her, but I'd forgotten. In the meantime, the tiny cat settled it for me. I was staying here for Christmas.

I carried Aunt Bitty's letter, along with her furry friend, into the sitting room. The fire had burned down somewhat. I picked up another log and threw it on top of the embers. Then I settled down in Bitty's rocking chair to read. Miss Skiffins chose the overstuffed chair across from me.

I slowly opened the envelope, noticing for the first time the lingering scent of Jean Nate. I began to read slowly, still afraid of the emotions I might experience through my aunt's last communication.

My dearest Ivy:
 If you're reading this letter it is because I am gone. I would tell you not to cry, but I know you will. You must remember, though, that I am with my Father, and my

joy is overflowing. If you are sad, it is because we will have to miss each other for a while. As I write this, that seems almost too difficult to bear. But I know that once I am in His presence, sorrow will vanish. I am counting on that.

By now you've discovered that I've left you my bookstore. You're probably wondering why. It is because no one could possibly love it more than you do. It is important that you know, however, that I do not require you to run it. You are free to do whatever you want to do. You may sell it or you may stay. That is entirely up to you.

Many years ago I came to Winter Break with a broken heart. I was at a loss to find my place in the world. Although I originally came to visit my best friend, Emily Steiff, I fell in love with the town. With money my father sent me, I decided to buy the building that now houses the bookstore. Back then it was just an old house that needed a lot of fixing up. Working on it became therapy for me. I still wonder how it turned into a bookstore. It was as if the house always knew what it was supposed to be. One day it was a house, and the next day, it was a bookstore.

Everyone thought I was crazy to stay in

Winter Break, including my parents, your grandparents, and your mother. But for the first time, I felt I had found the place I belonged. I was home. And so I stayed.

Now you're in Winter Break, perhaps at your own crossroads. You are not alone. Dewey and Amos will do everything they can to help you. Also remember what Pastor Taylor says: "The goodness of God gives me strength."

God has never let me down, Ivy. Never. I have failed Him many times, but His love for me is constant and unchanging.

So, my beautiful Ivy, I want you to know this: I count it a privilege to have been your "Grape Aunt Bitty." The truth is, you have always been more like a daughter to me. I believe you understand me more than anyone ever has. I always felt that someday you would come back to Winter Break, but perhaps that was just the silly wish of an old woman.

God has a plan for you, my darling. You will find it. I have no doubt of that.

Love God, love people, live life, and always forgive. Even yourself. These are the guideposts of my life and they've never led me the wrong way. They will also light your path.

I have faith in you.

All my love,
Bitty (Mark 12:30–31)

PS: Remember, some people spend their whole lives searching for something that is standing right in front of them.

Bitty was right about the crying. In fact, I had a really good boo-hoo fest. Even Miss Skiffins opened one of her eyes to see what the ballyhoo was all about.

Bitty was telling me that she loved me and that she wasn't blaming me for not visiting her before she died. Her concern was that I forgive myself. For her, I would try. But right now, it felt impossible. How did my priorities get so upside down that I forgot what was most important? My fear of being Ivy shouldn't have been more important than my love for my aunt.

I sat and rocked for quite a while, thinking. What was it about Bitty that had allowed her to see her path so clearly? Why hadn't I found mine? I asked God to open up His plan for me. "My aunt Bitty seems to think you have a place for me, Father," I whispered. "Help me to find my way. Please."

Finally, I got up to go to bed. I was looking forward to going to church in the morning. Many of my old friends would be there. And I'd get to see Pastor Taylor again. He was very special to me. I'd never connected to any pastor the way I had to him.

I carried Bitty's letter over to the desk and opened the drawer to place it inside. Because it was dark and I couldn't clearly see the lock, I turned on the old desk lamp. Although I'd seen Bitty's notepad sitting near her phone more than once, the way the light shone on it made it look like there was writing on it. I put my envelope inside the drawer, locked it again, and picked up the notepad. Although they hadn't been obvious in the light of day, I was now able to see indentions on the top sheet of paper. I grabbed a pencil from the holder on the desk and began to lightly scribble across the top of the page, using the side of the pencil lead. You know, like something someone might see on one of those CSI shows on TV. Not that I would know anything about that, of course.

Slowly, the words began to take shape. It was one of Bitty's lists. When I finished, I put the pencil down and held the piece of paper directly under the desk light.

Wednesday
1. I — PO
2. Pack t.c.
3. D — coming here?
4. BM for I — Don't forget!
5. DRL — chk
6. W clk
7. Put c in o
8. O — extra? Call
9. Ivy. Call?
10. PT — Ap W?

I'd forgotten my aunt's way of making lists. They were written in her own brand of shorthand. No one but Bitty could decipher her notes. I think she liked it that way. But this list was written on Wednesday, the day she died. Could there be something here that could lead us to the truth?

I carefully tore off the top sheet of paper, opened the desk drawer again, put the list inside, and relocked the drawer. Maybe this would help us to find the person who killed Bitty. I'd tell Amos about it tomorrow.

As I stood up and reached over to turn off the lamp, I thought I saw something move at the window. It spooked me so much, a small shriek escaped through my lips before I could stop myself. Was someone out there? Watching me?

I walked slowly toward the window and looked out. All I could see was the falling snow and the empty street, highlighted by the glow of the streetlamp. Had I imagined it?

I lowered the shade and began climbing the stairs toward Bitty's apartment. The shadow at the window only added to my growing apprehension. The same feeling of being watched that I'd experienced that morning had returned — in spades. Either my imagination was out of control, or someone was worried about me. Or what I might find out.

I called Miss Skiffins, and she came running up the stairs. We climbed into bed, and she cuddled next to me until I fell asleep. I dreamed that Aunt Bitty was alive and hiding somewhere in Winter Break.

But no one would tell me where she was.

8

I woke up Sunday morning feeling decid-
edly cranky. Lying in bed, reminding myself,
"This is the day the Lord has made. I will
rejoice and be glad in it," helped. My
mother started every day repeating that
verse over and over. I think it gave her the
strength to make it to her first cup of coffee. Actually, I really admired her for her
commitment to enjoying the life God had
given her. "Ivy," she'd say when I was in a
bad mood, "God made this day just for you.
He's placed blessings in your pathway. If
you don't look for them, you might miss
them."

Even though I was frustrated by a lack of
sleep and concerns over finding out the
truth about Bitty, I was looking forward to
church. It had been a long time since I'd
been able to attend a service at Winter
Break's Faith Community Church. When I
was younger, it seemed as if Pastor Ephraim

Taylor was able to see straight into my soul. His sermons applied to my life, and I always left church feeling that God had spoken something personally to me. Aunt Bitty told me that Pastor Taylor had the ability to speak "a word in due season." For a while, I thought it had something to do with the time of the year, but eventually I figured out that it meant he was so surrendered to God, the Holy Spirit could lead him to preach exactly what people needed to hear.

I repeated the rejoicing scripture one more time and rolled out of bed. I almost knocked a surprised Miss Skiffins right off the covers and onto the floor. After calming her and finding my slippers, we made our way to the kitchen. I fed her, put on some coffee, then got dressed for church.

Church had always been an integral part of Winter Break. A little over half the town attended Faith Community. Another ninety or so were members of the First Mennonite Church down by the river. Actually, the original name of the church was Gutenberg First Mennonite Church, but no one in Winter Break used the *Gutenberg* part anymore. Most of the church members were part of the Baumgartner family that migrated from Gutenberg, Germany. The original Baumgartners were German immigrants who took up farming after settling in Winter Break several generations ago. Heirs of the great-grandchildren and the great-great-grandchildren still lived in Winter Break and continued to farm the family land. Once in a while, a brave Baumgartner escaped Winter Break, but for the most part, these deserters were dismissed as lost lambs who had unfortunately succumbed to the call of the world. After the shock of their betrayal wore off, their names were never mentioned again. Eventually, it was as if they'd never existed — unless of course they came back. Then all was forgiven and the duly chastened Baumgartner took his or her rightful place back in the bosom of the family.

Although some churches might feel somewhat competitive with each other, especially in a small town, this was not the case in Winter Break. Everyone at Faith Community understood that First Mennonite was a family church with a long-standing tradition, and the members of First Mennonite understood that most people who weren't related to them might feel more comfortable at Faith Community. For the most part, the churches worked together as one body as the scriptures taught. However, everyone realized that while some members were arms, legs, or feet, about ninety of them were Baumgartners.

In a town of a little over six hundred citizens, that left quite a few people who had no church home. They were, of course, considered to be fields ready for harvest, and both groups did everything they could to bring in the sheaves, regardless of what church they ended up in. Unfortunately, some of these "sheaves" weren't interested in coming in and were quite vocal about it. But Christians in Winter Break had no intention of giving up. The fields would be plucked before Judgment Day, and that's all there was to it. I suspected, although no one would ever admit it, that somewhere there was an unofficial tabulation being kept and that many of the town's faithful believed that sitting near the Great White Throne was a tall trophy made of pure gold, waiting to be awarded to the Winter Break church that won the Salvation Super Bowl. I kind of doubted that God saw it that way. The important thing was that Winter Break Christians were committed to preaching the Word, whether their targets thought they needed to hear it or not.

I checked my makeup, grabbed my purse, and was on my way down the stairs when someone knocked on the front door. At first

I couldn't tell who it was because his back was turned, but when I opened the door, I found Amos standing on the steps, dressed in a dark blue suit and a black trench coat. It was the first time I'd seen him in anything besides his uniform since I'd arrived in Winter Break. I'd forgotten how attractive he could be.

"Thought I'd drive you to church, Ivy," he said. "If that's okay."

For some reason, I suddenly felt shy, but I mumbled something about appreciating his thoughtfulness. Within a few minutes, I was safely ensconced in his patrol car, and we were on our way to church.

Since Winter Break is a pretty small town, I had only a few minutes to tell him about Aunt Bitty's list and the note from Olivia. I also told him a little bit about my dinner with Noel, but at the last minute, I decided not to tell him about finding Noel going through the boxes of books. It wasn't that I wanted to keep it a secret, but I didn't think he would be objective about Noel, and I hadn't made up my mind about him yet. I didn't want someone else doing my thinking for me. Amos and I agreed to go back to Bitty's after lunch and look at the list together.

As we pulled into the church parking lot,

I noticed that several men from the church were waiting to help anyone who needed a little support across the snow-covered parking lot. It was obvious that an attempt had been made to clear it, but last night's snow had added another slippery layer.

"Wait a minute. I'll come around and get you," Amos said as he parked the car. I wasn't used to being treated like a helpless woman, so I ignored his comment and opened my door. I no sooner stepped out of the car than I felt my feet slip out from underneath me. Thankfully, Amos was able to grab me before I landed smack on my derriere. He held me while I got my balance. Being so close felt funny — but nice. Then I looked up into his face and saw something familiar. It was the same look he'd had the day he left to go to live with his father. I'd almost forgotten about it. "I guess there's really nothing for me here, Ivy," he'd said before he got on the bus for Oklahoma. "Mama's married again. She and her new husband are moving to California. I don't want to live with them, and no one in this town cares anything about me."

The pressure of Amos's arms around me brought me back to the present. "I swear, Ivy Towers," he said softly, "you must not know that scripture about a haughty spirit going before a fall. Why are you so contrary?"

I struggled out of his embrace. "I'm not contrary, Amos Parker. I'm just stubborn." I had to smile. "Sorry. Guess I'm just not used to such gentlemanly conduct. I'll do better next time."

He chuckled and shook his head. "Like there's ever going to be a next time."

I reached over and took his arm. "Now, now. Let's not get an attitude." I pulled out my best Scarlet O'Hara voice. "Why, kind sir, if you would be so considerate as to escort me into the church, I would be eternally grateful."

He rolled his eyes. "Now you're overdoing it."

I batted my eyelashes at him. "So sorry."

He grunted but couldn't conceal a smile. We trudged through the snow and finally made it to the church entrance. A man swung the door open for us.

"O–Odie?" I stuttered. "Odie Rimrucker?"

It was Odie all right, but instead of greasy hair flying every which way and soiled, mismatched clothing, this Odie was neat and clean with slicked-back hair, a nice suit, and a sparkle in his eye.

"Why, Ivy Towers," he said with a big grin, "I heard you was back. It's been a long time, girl. My goodness gracious, you look jes' the same as you did when you was little. Pretty red hair and all." He reached out and locked me in a big bear hug. I was too surprised to react. Was this really Odorous Odie?

After he let me go and I caught my breath, I greeted him with a smile and a "Nice to see you, too." After we'd walked a few feet past him, I asked Amos about him.

"I'll tell you about it after church," he whispered. "It's quite a story."

As we entered the sanctuary, I saw several familiar faces. Emily Baumgartner, one of the friends I'd made during my excursions to Winter Break, waved and started toward me. But before she could reach me and I could ask her what a Baumgartner was doing away from the family church, a thin, bejeweled hand grabbed my arm. I turned to see a middle-aged woman with a hat almost bigger than she was, smiling at me sweetly.

"You must be little Ivy," she said in a soft, high-pitched voice. "Your dear, dear aunt talked about you all the time."

I felt Amos's hand on my shoulder. "Ivy, this is Lila Hatcher, your aunt's best friend."

Tears filled the woman's large, hazy blue eyes. "That's the truth, dear. She was my trusted friend and confidante. I don't know what I'm going to do without her. I hope you'll stay here and carry on her legacy. I'm sure we can become friends, too."

She held out her hand, and I took it. Her skin was like soft leather, and I could feel the remnants of hand cream clinging to it. "Thank you," I said. "Unfortunately, I'm just here to make her final arrangements and close the bookstore. I'll be going back to school in January."

Her eyes widened. "Oh, my dear," she said. "I hope you'll change your mind. I can't imagine Winter Break without our bookstore."

"I'm sorry." I didn't want to be rude, but Emily was waiting to greet me, and the service was about to start. "Maybe we can visit some other time when we're not so rushed."

"Please, dear," Lila said, "I would like to host an open house after the funeral tomorrow. Say about two thirty? Would that be all right with you? That will allow all of Bitty's friends to gather together and extend their condolences."

The idea of a social gathering hadn't occurred to me, but it was a good idea. "Thank you, Ms. Hatcher. I think that would be very nice."

"It's Lila, honey," she said, patting my arm. "I'm so glad. It gives me a chance to do something for Bitty. We'll talk more when there's time." Her eyes flushed with tears once more as she turned and walked away.

I felt a tap on the back and turned to see Emily smiling at me. "Oh, Ivy," she said. "I'm so glad to see you, but I'm so sorry it had to be like this."

She wrapped her arms around me and hugged me tightly. I'd forgotten what good friends we'd been. I was beginning to see that I'd forgotten a lot of things about Winter Break.

I gently pulled myself out of her arms. "Okay," I said. "You have to tell me how in the world a Baumgartner wound up at Faith Community. Did you defect, or were you kicked out?"

She laughed in a light, lilting way that brought back warm summer days spent sitting on the dock at Lake Winter Break, talking about boys and life in general.

"Neither one, smarty-pants. The only way a Baumgartner escapes the fold is to quit being a Baumgartner." She held up her left hand and wiggled her fingers, one of which sported a wedding ring.

"Emily! Who . . ."

Before I had a chance to finish my question, Buddy Taylor, Pastor Taylor's son, stepped up behind Emily and put his hands on her shoulders. "Was brave enough to take on the Baumgartner clan?" he finished. "You get one guess."

Buddy planted a kiss on the top of Emily's head, which wasn't difficult since Buddy was over six feet tall and Emily was exactly five feet and one-half inch. I knew this because she had lamented the fact constantly. She'd always wanted to leave Winter Break and become a model. Unfortunately, not many agencies were looking for models of Emily's stature.

I laughed. "Congratulations, you two." I slapped Buddy lightly on the arm. "If I remember right, you teased poor Emily every chance you could get. What was that all about?"

He wrapped his arms around his beaming wife. "When you're a kid, it's hard to tell a girl you're crazy about her. I guess the only way I could get her attention was by being a big pain in the —"

"Buddy!" Emily whispered. "Don't you say that word in church."

"Neck? What's wrong with saying 'neck' in church?" Buddy asked innocently.

Emily shook her head while Amos and I

tried not to laugh. People were starting to stare.

"Okay, okay, I give," Buddy said. "But Amos knows what I mean, don't you, Amos?"

I looked at Amos just in time to see him flush the color of an overripe tomato. He pushed me lightly from behind. "We'll see you two later," he said gruffly. "There's Pastor Taylor. The service is getting ready to start."

We found a couple of seats a few pews from the front. Pastor Taylor seated himself on a chair next to the back wall on the small stage. Faith Community always had a rather long praise and worship service before the sermon. Pastor Taylor said he liked to step into the pulpit after praise had saturated the sanctuary. It made preaching much easier.

A young woman about my age stepped up and took the microphone. I didn't know her. Then three more people took the tiny platform. A young man of about seventeen or eighteen sat at the drums, and Bev Taylor, Pastor Taylor's wife, took her place at the piano. The woman at the podium encouraged us all to stand up.

As the strains of "Awesome God" began, I felt myself drawn immediately into worship. I felt as if God had stepped into the sanctuary with us. The worship leader took us through several wonderful songs, including some of my favorite old hymns, and then wrapped up her portion of the service with a song I'd never heard before. The words so touched my heart that when we were finished, I was surprised to find tears on my face. The words echoed in my heart. *"I'm desperate for you . . . lost without you."* How long had it been since I'd felt desperate for God? School seemed to take all my time and concentration. Had I substituted it for God's presence?

Amos handed me a tissue, and I wiped my face as we sat down. I really liked my church in Wichita. I had friends there, but school kept me from attending regularly. I had to admit to myself that even when I *was* in church, I never experienced this kind of worship.

Pastor Taylor made a few announcements; then he stopped and looked at me. "We are all aware that Bitty Flanagan went home to be with her Lord this week," he said. "Although we will definitely miss her wonderful spirit, we rejoice to know that she is safely in the arms of God. We're happy to have her niece, Ivy, home again. I hope you will all get a chance to tell her how much Bitty meant to us." His voice trembled as he finished the last part of his sentence.

I heard sniffs and muffled sobs throughout the room. My goodness, Bitty had certainly touched the lives of the people in Winter Break. It was amazing.

"Bitty's memorial service will be here tomorrow at one o'clock. Following the service, Lila Hatcher will host an open house at her home. She encourages everyone who knew Bitty to come by for some food and good memories. It will give all of us a chance to let Ivy know how special Bitty was to us and how glad we are to have her home.

"One other thing. Bitty and I talked once about her funeral. She told me she didn't want a bunch of flowers sitting around dying on her account. It was her wish that people give a memorial gift to the church instead of sending flowers. I think we should do what she said, but I, for one, intend to do both." His voice broke. "My family is giving a check to the missionary fund in her name, and we already called the Flower Market in Hugoton and ordered the most beautiful display we could afford." He took a handkerchief from his pocket and blew his nose. "I think Bitty Flanagan should go out in style. You all do whatever you feel led to do, but I hope you go out of your way to honor her in the best way you can."

A chorus of amens and hallelujahs rang out in the church. I felt as if the entire town of Winter Break had wrapped its arms around me in a big hug. Their love for Bitty had translated right over to me. I was so moved, it took me a few minutes to refocus myself on Pastor Taylor's sermon. I picked up his words just in time to hear him say:

"Jeremiah chapter 29, verse 11, says: 'For I know the plans I have for you,' declares the Lord, . . . 'plans to give you hope and a future.' " He closed his Bible and stepped in front of the pulpit.

"God, the creator of heaven and earth, is thinking about *you*," he said. "In fact, He planned for you even before you were born. You are not some generality bouncing around in life without purpose. The future He has planned for you isn't anything to be afraid of. It is full of His blessings. It will fulfill all the desires of your heart. How can you trust this? Because God made you. Only He knows what will truly bring you joy. But it requires something from you. A sacrifice."

He walked back to his pulpit and picked up his Bible. "Matthew 10:39 tells us what that sacrifice is along with what it will cost and what you will receive in return. 'Whoever finds his life will lose it, and whoever loses his life for my sake will find it.' "

Pastor Taylor paused and gazed at the crowd seated in the sanctuary. "The only way we will ever find the life God has prepared for us is to lay our lives on the altar. What is keeping you from giving all of your life to God?"

As he continued his sermon, his words kept running around in my head. Was I really living for God? Why couldn't I find the path God had for me? My parents wanted me to come to China and minister with them. Maybe that really was my calling. There wasn't any other opportunity in my life that presented me with a chance to do so much good for other people.

Then there was the job offer in Denver. It would be a chance to make something successful out of my life. I could be *Sam* there. I could leave Ivy behind forever. I'd wanted that for a long, long time.

I didn't get much more out of Pastor Taylor's sermon because I wasn't listening. I spent the rest of the time trying to figure out what God wanted from me. Could He have sent Noel Spivey to Winter Break?

As I mentally bounced back and forth between Denver and China, I felt confusion. If God was trying to tell me something,

I sure wasn't getting it.

A nudge from Amos's elbow reminded me that I needed to be listening instead of daydreaming. Pastor Taylor gave the closing prayer and dismissed us. As I turned to go, I found myself surrounded by Faith Community Church members. I knew most of them, but there were a few new faces in the crowd. Dewey talked to Amos while I focused on the other people around me. After they had all offered their condolences and exited the sanctuary, I finally saw Isaac Holsapple. He was standing off to the side of the sanctuary, watching me. His thin face, long nose, and dark, darting eyes had always reminded me of a weasel. His thinning hair was just as unkempt as always, but there wasn't as much of it left. Isaac was growing older. Odd that I'd never thought of him as either young or old. He never seemed to change. He was just Isaac.

We stared at each other for a few seconds. I made a move toward him, and he scampered out the door without speaking.

"Amos," I said quietly, glancing around the room to make sure no one remained. "Why is Isaac hiding from me? If he's innocent, why won't he talk to me?"

Amos shook his head. "I can't answer that, Ivy. I've known Isaac all my life. He's an

153

odd duck, but I've never seen him harm anyone. I think he's just really shy around people."

I picked up my coat and Bible from the pew. "Did Bitty ever say anything about him to you?" I asked.

Amos took my coat and held it up so that I could slip my arms in the sleeves. "No," he said thoughtfully. "Now that you mention it, she didn't talk much about him at all. I always thought it was a little odd. Not that your aunt gossiped about people; she didn't. But with Isaac, she seemed especially secretive."

When we reached the front lobby, we found Pastor Taylor and his wife standing near the front door.

"Ivy!" Pastor Taylor said loudly. "I'm so glad to see you. It's been a few years now, hasn't it?"

"About three," I said.

Bev reached out to hug me. "Oh, Ivy. When I look at you, I see Bitty. You two are so alike."

Pastor Taylor shook hands with Amos. "I hope you're taking good care of our girl here," he said.

Amos chuckled. "As much as I can, Pastor. Our Ivy has become quite independent."

"Honey, is there anything we can do for

you?" Bev asked. "Anything at all?"

"No," I said. Then something occurred to me. "Well, maybe there is."

Encouraged by the look on their faces, I took a deep breath and dove in. "Bitty was cremated, you know. And . . . I . . . I'm not sure what to do with her ashes. Elmer said something about keeping them in the store, but unless someone buys the whole store and keeps it open, that isn't going to work. Could . . . could you take them after the service tomorrow? I know you'll do the right thing. I don't want to take Bitty's remains with me. I think she needs to stay here in Winter Break."

I saw them exchange glances. "Sure, Ivy," Pastor Taylor said with a frown. "If that's what you want us to do."

I nodded, feeling relieved. "Yes, please. I can't leave without knowing this has been settled."

Amos grabbed my elbow. "I'm starving," he said. "We need to get to Ruby's before all the fried chicken is gone."

I said my good-byes to the Taylors while Amos steered me out the door. When we got to Ruby's, the place was packed. We had to wait about ten minutes for a table. The way Amos acted, you'd think he hadn't eaten for a year.

The only thing Ruby served on Sundays was her pan-fried chicken along with mashed potatoes and chicken gravy, green beans with bacon, rolls, and peach cobbler with ice cream for dessert. For one price, you got all you could eat. Sunday protocol consisted of stuffing yourself at Ruby's then heading home for a long Sunday afternoon nap. That was about all you could do when you were full of Ruby's chicken. Sleeping through a major part of the digestion process was your only protection.

The wives in Winter Break loved their Sunday routine. It meant that their husbands would ask for something "light" for dinner, if they asked for anything at all.

I knew we had work to do that afternoon, so with great effort I kept myself to two pieces of chicken and one helping of everything else. It wasn't easy. Ruby's flaky, butter-crusted entrée left the Colonel's chicken lying like roadkill in its path.

Between bites I asked Amos about Odie Rimrucker.

Amos wiped his mouth with his napkin, took a sip of coffee, and gazed forlornly at the food still sitting on his plate. Taking a break was a costly sacrifice, but he took it like a man. "You remember the mess Odie used to be?"

I nodded. Odie was as low class as you could be in Winter Break. No matter what your problem was, you could always comfort yourself with the knowledge that you were better off than Odie.

"You also remember that after Morley Watson died, Odie claimed he'd never drink again?"

I nodded again. "That happened a little over three years ago. Did he keep his promise?"

Amos picked up his fork in readiness for the end of the story. I guess it paid to be prepared. "He stopped for a while, but then one Friday night, he wandered over to Hiram Ledbetter's and came back with a jar of 'medicine.'"

Winter Break had no bars, and Dewey refused to sell alcohol in his store. This forced those who imbibed to either purchase their supplies in Hugoton or buy a jar of Ledbetter's Life-Preserving Liniment. I never understood the name since no one ever suggested that you rub the stuff on your skin. In fact, there may have been a warning about contact with human flesh. But few people in town called it what it really was — moonshine, plain and simple. Deputy Watson warned Hiram more than once about his illegal still, but Hiram moved the thing around so much, it was tough to find. After awhile, Deputy Watson gave up. Most people in town acted as if they had no idea that Ledbetter's Liniment was hundred proof. Perhaps it was easier than admitting that Hiram Ledbetter was craftier than the law in Winter Break.

"Did he drink it?" I asked.

"Yep. In fact, he drank so much, he passed out for two whole days. Old Doc Evans came over from Hugoton and checked him out. He said that all we could do was let Odie sleep. Doc said he'd either live or die. It was in God's hands."

"My goodness," I said. "Did anyone keep an eye on him?"

Amos actually released the death grip on his fork a little. "This is the interesting part, the part you don't know. Someone watched over him all right. It was Bitty. She took him in. Let him sleep it off. When he finally started to stir, she nursed him back to consciousness. No one knows what happened after that, Ivy, but after four days with Bitty, Odie Rimrucker walked out of her place a different man. He got cleaned up, went back to church, and has been on the wagon ever since."

It was my turn to forget about Ruby's chicken. "Bitty never told me anything about that."

Amos smiled and shook his head. "She wouldn't. Bitty didn't believe in blabbing about her good deeds. You know that."

Yes, I knew that all right. She'd done many wonderful things for me. Good deeds that even my parents didn't know about. I'd always been able to tell her everything, without fear of condemnation.

"You have no idea what she said to Odie that made him quit drinking?"

Amos shook his head. "No. Even Pastor Taylor asked him about it, but Odie wouldn't say anything. He said it was something private between him and Bitty."

I stuck a bite of mashed potatoes in my mouth, but I was really chewing over Amos's story. Bitty had never been a drinker. What did she do that no one else had been able to do? Odie had been preached to, scolded, locked up, loved on, forgiven, and prayed over for more than twenty years. Now that Bitty was gone, I'd probably never know.

Amos took my silence and my forkful of Ruby's creamy whipped potatoes as a sign that he was free to pick up where he'd left off. He chomped into another chicken breast with a gusto that was usually reserved for cheering on his favorite basketball team, the Wichita State Shockers. Amos's perfect day would consist of sitting in front of his TV in his grody sweats, watching the Shockers, and munching on Ruby's chicken, followed by two or three pieces of her peach cobbler. I loved the Shockers, too, but a little popcorn was all I could handle. Whenever I got too excited, I'd yell and spit popcorn out of my mouth. It was a lot easier to clean up popcorn than pieces of greasy chicken.

When he took a breath, I saw it as an opportunity to ask the one question that had been burning in my mind ever since I got the phone call about Bitty's death. "Amos," I said, "why Bitty? She was such a good woman. She did so many wonderful things — why did she have to die?"

Amos put down his fork, allowing it to rest a moment. His hazel eyes locked on mine. "I don't know, Ivy, but my guess is that she trusted the wrong person. What's that scripture about being as wise as serpents and as harmless as doves? Your aunt trusted everyone. Unfortunately, not everyone *should* be trusted."

Although Amos's words made sense to me, I couldn't wrap my mind around why anyone would want to hurt Bitty Flanagan. What could have led someone to kill her? Was it something they wanted, or was it something she'd done?

Amos went back to his chicken. I watched him eat, glad he was enjoying his dinner, and even happier that I wasn't alone in my quest for justice.

I pushed Amos out of Ruby's around one thirty. He resisted, but I prevailed. Ruby seemed forlorn about my resistance to second helpings of everything, but I wanted to get back to the bookstore and examine Bitty's list. Besides, I'd run into Elmer, and he'd agreed to let me do some research on his computer. I had to meet him at the funeral home at five o'clock.

It was almost two by the time I made some coffee in an attempt to keep Amos awake. We sat upstairs in the kitchen so no one passing by the bookstore could see us. I didn't need Sunday visitors interrupting our research.

I handed a piece of paper to Amos. "This isn't the original list," I said. "I wrote this out so it would be easier to read."

He looked through it carefully. "Okay," he said. "Let's go through these one by one. Maybe we'll see something that will help us."

I read the first entry: *"I — PO."*

"Easy," Amos said. "Isaac — post office. We know that he did that on Wednesdays."

161

"Great." I put a check mark next to it. "Pack *t.c.*"

Amos thought for a minute. "Well, the church was having a dinner that night. Could *t.c.* stand for something she was planning to take? Something that starts with a *T* and something else that starts with a *C?*"

I shook my head. "She would have written *t* and *c* if there were two things." I ran the letters through my mind a few times. "I've got it! It's *tablecloth.* I'll bet she was going to take my grandmother's tablecloth."

I got up and started rummaging through the kitchen. In one of the bottom drawers, I found what I was looking for. I held up the large Irish linen tablecloth embroidered with harps and starlings. I'd always been amazed that Bitty actually used it. I was afraid it would get stained and ruined. "Nonsense," Bitty said when I told her my feelings. "My mother worked hard on it. She created this beautiful tablecloth from her heart. When I share it with others, I'm sharing her. What's the point of having it if it's not used?"

"I recognize that," Amos said. "She brought it to every one of our church dinners."

"Well, we can mark that off our list." I slid the tablecloth back into the drawer. "Too bad it won't be used again," I said softly. "Bitty loved it so."

Amos frowned at me as I sat down next to him. "Won't be used again? What do you mean? It's yours now, Ivy. You'll use it."

I sighed with exasperation. "Why do I keep forgetting that? I know in my head that Bitty's things belong to me, but somewhere in my heart, I can't accept it."

Amos grunted. "I don't have enough time to explain *that* to you today. Maybe you should think about it yourself."

He picked up his pen and checked number two off the list. I wasn't sure what he meant by his comment, but I had the distinct feeling it wasn't a compliment. I felt a slight rush of anger. Why wasn't Amos more understanding? He knew I loved Bitty. Before I could build my resentment up a little more, he read off the next entry on our list.

"D — coming here?" He put the pen down. "That's easy, too. *D* is for Dewey. She was wondering if Dewey was coming to pick her up for the church supper."

I crossed my arms and sat back in my chair. "How do you know this note was about the church supper?"

Amos looked confused. "What do you mean?"

"Amos, this is the first clue we have about someone coming here on the day Bitty died."

Amos's eyebrows shot up in amusement. "You surely don't suspect Dewey Tater. That's ridiculous. Dewey wouldn't hurt anyone, especially your aunt."

"Look," I said, shaking my head, "I feel funny bringing this up, but aren't we supposed to look at the evidence logically? Without emotion?" I leaned over closer to him. "Why did Bitty postpone their wedding? What was it that changed her mind? What if she knew something about Dewey — something he couldn't risk having anyone else find out? Or what if he felt rejected and killed her in a crime of passion?"

Amos whooped with laughter. "Dewey Tater? A crime of passion? Holy cow, Ivy. Have you ever even met Dewey?"

I had to admit that it sounded silly, but I was determined to find Bitty's killer — no matter what. "Look, Amos," I said, fighting to keep my temper in check, "we can't rule out anybody. Even Dewey. Now let's move on."

We continued with the list, trying to solve the rest of Bitty's cryptic messages. I was pretty sure number seven was a note to put a casserole in the oven for the church dinner, but except for number nine, which was obviously a note to call me, we couldn't decipher anything else. I quickly wrote out another copy of the list for Amos.

"Take this with you," I said. "Maybe something will occur to you. I think we should concentrate on that particular Wednesday. We know Bitty's normal schedule, and we know there was a church dinner that night. Perhaps we'll interpret most of these entries if we focus on those two things."

Amos took the list from my hand. "You know, Ivy, there might not be anything here that will help us to find her killer."

I jabbed my finger at my list, still sitting on the table in front of me. "What about number nine?" I said. "Why was she planning to call me?"

He shook his head. "I'm not sure she was. There's a question mark next to the entry. She wasn't sure if she wanted to phone you or not."

"But that's just it, Amos. Why would she question that? She called me quite often. And I called her, too. Just because I hadn't been in town for a while didn't mean we didn't keep in touch."

He held up his hands in mock surrender. "Look, maybe she just wasn't sure she had time to call you on Wednesday. Maybe she was busy. I'm not saying you're wrong, Ivy. I just don't think we should jump to any conclusions based on this list."

"You've forgotten something very important," I said.

Amos looked at me with surprise. "And what would that be?"

"Was anything of Bitty's moved before I got here on Friday?"

Amos considered my question. "No. I don't think so. I tried to keep everything the way it was because of my initial suspicions."

"You didn't empty the trash? Anything like that?"

He shook his head slowly. "I came here and cleaned up the blood on the floor, but I threw the rags in a plastic bag and took that with me. I didn't want you to see them."

"Well then, Mister Deputy Sherriff, where is the original of this list? I've looked everywhere. It's not here."

His expression grew stormy. "Maybe Bitty threw it away somewhere else. And don't call me *Mister Deputy Sheriff*."

"Okay, okay. But where would she have disposed of the list? According to Isaac, she didn't go anywhere that morning. And anyway, this list has notes related to a dinner that was supposed to happen that night. That means she wouldn't be finished with it until after the dinner. It should be here, Amos."

Amos just stared at me. It was obvious he couldn't refute my logic.

"Someone took the list. Why? There must be something here that was too dangerous for her killer to leave behind. If we can figure it out, I think it will point right to him. We've got to keep at this until we understand each and every entry."

He stared at the list for a few moments. Finally, he looked up and scowled at me. "Ivy, it's possible you're right. It's also possible that you're putting way too much importance into this note. I hope we don't waste time on something that has nothing to do with why Bitty died."

I reached over and patted his hand. "I've got a feeling, Amos. I've just got a feeling —"

"Oh no," he responded, his worried expression deepening. "I remember when you used to tell me you 'had a feeling' when we were kids. Somehow or other, we always ended up in trouble."

I withdrew my hand. "I'm sure I have no idea what you're talking about."

"No idea what I'm talking about. Are you

kidding me?" He slapped his hand on the surface of the table. "What about the time you told me you 'had a feeling' that Lymon Penwordy was stealing cows from Newton Widdle? You made me sit out in a cold, wet cow pasture in the middle of the night, I might add, for over four hours so we could catch him at it."

I smiled as sweetly as I could before I said, "And I was right, wasn't I? We saw Lymon sneak three cows out of Newton's corral."

"Oh, you were certainly right," he snorted. " 'Course, it took years before Morley Watson quit telling the story of how I came running into his office the next morning hollerin', 'Deputy! I know who's been stealing all the Widdle cows!' "

It took all the fortitude I could muster not to giggle. Deputy Watson had arrested Lymon, but he'd chuckled all the way through it. I was told that after he loaded his prisoner into his car to drive him to the Stevens County Jail in Hugoton, he and Lymon were both laughing so hard you could still hear them — even after they'd left the city limits.

"And then there was the time you were convinced Sara Beasley's state fair award-winning jam was actually store-bought. 'I just have a feeling, Amos,' you said."

168

"And what's your point?" I asked as innocently as I could. "I was right about that, too."

"Yeah, you were right. But you weren't the one Ed Beasley threatened to stuff inside a Mason jar. I had to hide every time I saw him coming. Good thing they finally moved to Cawker City. I was finally able to walk the streets again instead of skulking around in the shadows."

"I think their daughter Mabel Mae lived in Cawker City," I said. "They probably moved there to be near her."

"They moved because they were too embarrassed to stay in Winter Break."

"Well, if they did, it isn't my fault," I replied with a sniff. "Sara's the one who cheated. Besides, Cawker City is a very nice place to live. I mean, they have that ball of twine and all."

Amos grunted. "Yes, I'm sure they moved to Cawker City because they have the world's largest ball of twine. Must be why so many people flock there."

"Cawker City is just about the same size as Winter Break," I said.

Amos raised one eyebrow. "And your point is?"

"Okay, look," I said. "I really think this list is important. If you don't, I can't do anything about that. But the truth is it's all we've got. I'm going to keep working on it."

Amos yawned, a sure sign that Ruby's chicken was finally kicking in. He stood up. "I'm going home to take a nap. I'll take the list with me and mull it over. When do we get together again?"

"I'm going to the funeral home this evening to do a little research on Elmer's computer. I've got to get some idea of how much these books are worth so I'll know whether Noel's offer is fair. I found an inventory list in Bitty's desk, but I still need to write down some information about the new books."

"Do you need help with that?" Amos asked.

I grinned at him. "You've got that dazed chicken look. I think you'd better lie down and recover. You're not much help to me in this state."

Amos stood up from the table. "I'm pretty sure you're referring to Ruby's chicken," he said wryly, "although I think you could have phrased that a little differently. What time are you going to Elmer's?"

I looked up at Aunt Bitty's red rooster clock on the wall over the oven. "I plan to get there around five," I said. "What time does church start tonight?"

"There isn't any service on Sunday nights anymore."

That surprised me. Sunday night church had been a Winter Break tradition for as long as I could remember. "What happened?" I asked.

"Most of our congregation is made up of farmers. You know they work six or seven days a week. Pastor Taylor decided that families needed some time together. Those who want to go to church Sunday nights go over to First Mennonite. The rest of them get to see their families before they head back to the fields." He shrugged. "I think it was an inspired idea."

"Well, I guess that gives me all the time I need to work on this tonight." I stood up and started toward the stairs, expecting Amos to follow me. Just as I reached the top step, Amos reached out and grabbed me. Startled, I turned to face him.

"Listen to me, Ivy," he said, his jaw tight, his eyes narrowed, "this isn't a story from one of those Nancy Drew books you used to read. You've got to be careful. If there is a killer hiding in Winter Break, and he feels you're a threat to him . . ."

"I'll be okay, Amos," I said, not feeling as brave as I sounded. "No one even knows we're suspicious. We'll find him. We're a good team."

"I hope you're right. But if at any time you feel unsafe, you've got to promise to call me right away."

"I promise."

His eyes were fastened on mine, and his grip softened to something close to a caress. For a moment, I wondered if he was going to kiss me, but instead, he let me go. He headed down the stairs and left, Bitty's bell signaling his departure.

I stood at the top of the steps, his words still ringing in my head. He was right. This wasn't a story in a novel, nor was it Newton Widdle's cows or Sara Beasley's jam.

This was the real thing, and we had to be careful. I couldn't control the little shiver that ran like cold water down my back.

9

A little before five o'clock, I left the book-store with Bitty's inventory records tucked safely under my arm, along with a list of the books from the new shipment. By matching some of the entries on the records with books on the shelves, I had deciphered Bitty's codes. *AS* meant the book was *actively stocked. SS* was *sold and shipped,* and *WS* meant *waiting to be shipped.* Thankfully, there were no outstanding books to be mailed. The entries stopped at the end of November. I was relieved to know that none of my aunt's customers were waiting for something they would never receive.

Since I'd been staying at Bitty's, I'd gotten four phone calls from book dealers. Their community proved to be a very tight-knit group, because after the last one, all the out-of-town calls abruptly ceased. I assumed the merchants had passed the word around about Bitty. All the other phone calls were from Winter Break people wanting to express their sorrow at my aunt's passing.

Alma had reminded me at church that I needed to come to the post office and pick up Bitty's mail, especially since there appeared to be so many condolence cards. I guessed that a lot of them would be from Bitty's customers. I made a mental note to go there tomorrow after the open house at Lila's. Maybe there would be something from the mysterious Olivia.

For now, though, I didn't really believe those new books were involved in Bitty's death. If someone wanted them, he could have gotten to them long ago. My only real worry was their value and how that would enter into any offer Noel might make for the inventory.

As I trudged the two blocks to Elmer's, I wondered if we were in for more precipitation. The streets were still snow packed, and the freezing temperatures weren't going to help them get cleared anytime soon. I could feel moisture in the chilly wind that whipped at my face, a sure sign of either frozen drizzle or more snow. My biggest fear was that bad weather would force some of Winter Break's rural residents to stay away from the memorial service tomorrow. I really wanted Bitty to have the kind of funeral she deserved.

I couldn't help but think about my mother, wondering if she shouldn't have made the effort to come to Winter Break. Bitty was her only aunt. My feelings wavered. I'd told her not to worry about it, but now that I was here by myself, I realized that a small seed of resentment had squirmed its way into my mind.

I was still mulling this over when Elmer opened the door for me. "Nice to see you again, Ivy," he said. Actually, he said, "Nice to tee you again, Ivy." I thought about saying *Nice to tee you, too,* but my mother had instilled good manners in me. Besides, Elmer was letting me use his computer.

He took me into his office, turned the computer on for me, and signed on to the Internet. "There's pop in the fridge, a coffeemaker in the break room next door, and the bathroom is just down the hall," he said.

I assured him I was fine and thanked him again for his help.

"I'm happy to help you in any way I can. My telephone number is right here on the desk. You know I live next door so I can be here in a flash if you need something."

I assured him that wouldn't be necessary, and with one last funeral home smile, he left me alone to tally up the worth of Bitty's timeworn empire.

I took off my coat and put it on the back of the rather lumpy padded desk chair. Then I set the inventory records next to the computer and pulled a notepad and pen from my purse. I scooted an old lamp teetering on the edge of Elmer's rickety desk next to the notepad and clicked on the light. The lamp's base was grimy and in desperate need of cleaning. The glass cover was also coated in dust. I took a tissue from my purse and cleaned away a little of the grunge. Underneath I found green, yellow, and blue leaves set against a gold-colored glass background. There was something else above it. I wasn't certain, but it looked like a bird of some kind. I couldn't help but wonder what was waiting underneath the neglect the years had deposited. I promised myself to clean it for Elmer when I had some extra time.

I started my search by looking for sites that dealt in rare books. I was happy to find that there were several search sites that covered thousands of books, old and new. When I ran up against a book that wasn't listed with a particular online location, I searched for the book by name. I usually found it listed with an auction company. Unfortunately, some of them didn't have prices, so those books took a little longer to research.

I quickly learned that condition was everything. Books were classified as *Very Fine, Fine, Near Fine, Very Good, Good,* and *Poor.* Some had dust jackets; some didn't. First editions were more valuable, but evaluating whether or not a book was a genuine first edition wasn't always easy. Pictures of the books were nice, but since I hadn't been able to drag the bookstore over to Elmer's, I had no idea of condition — or anything else.

After about two hours, I'd barely scratched the surface. What I had matched was pretty amazing. Although most of the books were in the two-hundred- to three-hundred-dollar range, several could be worth a great deal more, depending on their condition.

I leaned back in Elmer's threadbare chair, deciding that a cup of coffee was in order, but before I deserted my post for a caffeine break, I wanted to count how many pages I still had to go in the latest inventory book. If I could find most of the books on the Internet, I could at least make an educated guess about the total value of Bitty's treasured books. If not, I was going to be spending a lot of time in Elmer's funeral home. Although I wasn't really afraid, I had to admit that sitting by myself in these surroundings was a little creepy.

I flipped through the remaining pages, counting them quickly. As I reached the last one, I saw something that I hadn't noticed before. Between the final page with writing on it and the first blank page was a ragged strip of paper. I looked around the desk and found Elmer's magnifying glass. Then I pulled the lamp as close as possible and positioned the glass next to the open book. It was clear to me that a page was missing. I'd just assumed that the last entry on the back of the previous page was the end of the transactions. Had someone torn out some records in an attempt to hide something? Perhaps Bitty had made a mistake and wanted to start over. I realized right away, however, that if that were the case, the rejected page would have been before the final entry, not after. The missing page made my suspicions more real. Someone must have removed it *and* taken the list Bitty had written out and left on her desk.

I had just reached for the phone to call Amos, when I thought I heard a noise coming from somewhere inside the building. I waited a few seconds, but everything stayed quiet. I chalked it up to imagination and picked up the receiver. The tiny *bang* I'd heard before turned into a noisy crash. I definitely wasn't the only one here.

I put the receiver down and went to the door, glancing up and down the hallway, hoping to see Elmer trotting toward me. There was no one in sight.

"Elmer? Elmer, is that you?" My voice was at a higher-than-normal pitch. I sounded as frightened as I felt. I waited for an answer. Nothing. I had a couple of choices. I could either lock myself in the office and call for help or go plunging into the unknown, searching for the source of the racket just like they do in all those stupid horror movies. Not that I would know anything about that, of course. Since this definitely wasn't a movie, I slowly closed the door, turned the lock, and ran to the phone.

As I picked up the receiver, my mind flashed again to those dumb movies. I quickly repented for every single one I'd ever watched, but at that moment, some of the images were still floating around in my brain. For instance, right before the hapless victims found themselves facing certain death, they would invariably try to call for help. Of course, the phone never worked. I'd always wondered why they didn't just accept the fact that good old Ma Bell was programmed to snooze right before the insane murderer jumped out of the shadows. It would save time. Chiding myself for thinking that way, I grabbed the receiver. No dial tone. I'm not kidding. I pounded on the phone with my fist several times, figuring that somehow the silent instrument would interpret this as a very serious request and the dial tone would magically spring to life. It didn't.

Funny the stuff that goes through your mind when you imagine the worst. Probably the smartest thing for me to do would be to sit in Elmer's office until someone found me. I knew Elmer would be back sometime in the morning to take Bitty's ashes over to the church. What bothered me most was the possibility that I wouldn't have time to take a shower and dress before the service. It was probably ridiculous, but I was horrified to think I would let Aunt Bitty down in the very last thing I would ever be able to do for her. I had on jeans and a sweatshirt, and my hair was in ponytails. I couldn't possibly show up looking like this. The other thing that worried me was the realization that my staying here might be just what the killer wanted. I was isolated, easy to get to. The thought made me feel frightened and helpless. And that made me mad.

So I made a decision to make a frenzied dash out the front door and run to Elmer's house. Then I remembered the part in the movie where the heroine runs to the person she expects to help her only to find out that he is the murderer. I rolled that over in my mind a few times, but I honestly couldn't imagine poor Elmer killing anyone. The idea of the timid little funeral director pointing a gun at me and yelling, "Top or I'll toot!" didn't seem to fit my horror movie fantasy. That picture in my head was the thing that made me decide to run toward the known and away from the unknown.

I unlocked the door to the office and slowly opened it. I looked down the hall to my left and didn't see anything. Then I looked toward my right, in the direction of the front door. The coast was clear. I could either creep slowly down the hall, giving whoever was in the building plenty of time to catch up to me, or I could run as fast as I could, push open the front doors, and skedaddle to Elmer's house. I took a deep breath, prayed, and took off like Freddy Krueger was hot on my tail. As I neared the front doors, I heard something behind me. I could swear it was someone calling my name. I had no intention of turning around and letting Freddy catch up to me. Instead,

I ran faster, holding my arms out to push the street-side door open so I could make my escape. But instead of ending up on the sidewalk outside, I felt something hard hit me on the head. The last thing I remembered before the darkness took over was the sense that someone stood behind me, whispering my name.

10

Having never been knocked unconscious before, I was of the opinion that people thus affected would eventually wake up without any memory of their brief visit to the state of oblivion. However, this wasn't my experience. I dreamed that someone was still chasing me. So when I opened my eyes and realized that a man whose face I couldn't clearly see was kneeling over me, touching me, I reacted in the most rational way possible. I decked him.

When he screeched, "Ow!" and put his hand to his nose, I realized I'd just smashed my fist into Amos's face.

"I see you're okay," Amos said crossly, rubbing his offended appendage. "But why did you hit me?"

I struggled to sit up. Elmer stood behind Amos, looking slightly relieved that he was out of range.

"What are you doing here?" I touched my

tender forehead. A sizable bump greeted me, along with one whale of a headache.

Amos slipped his hands under my armpits and helped me to my feet. "I came by to check on you," he said. "When I looked through the front door, I saw you lying on the floor. I ran over to Elmer's so he could let me in. And once again, if I may ask, why did you hit me?"

I wasn't as concerned about his bruised ego as I was about my narrow escape from disaster. "Someone was in here, Amos. Whoever it was cut the phone lines, chased me when I tried to run out, and whacked me over the head. You must have come just in time and scared him away."

My dramatic revelation didn't produce the reaction I'd expected. Instead of throwing their arms around me in a grateful expression of overwhelming joy that I had escaped an early grave, I saw Amos and Elmer exchange a quick glance. Their expressions reminded me of the time my mother made homemade lemonade and forgot to add sugar.

"What's the deal?" I asked, feeling more than a little miffed by their seeming lack of compassion. "You believe me, don't you? Someone was after me. How do you think I got bashed on the head?"

Amos put his arm around my shoulders and guided me to one of the tired-looking overstuffed chairs in the lobby. "First of all, I want you to sit down," he said. "You still look a little shaky."

Either he was right or the room was actually spinning. I gently lowered myself into the chair, holding my head so that it wouldn't move any more than absolutely necessary.

"Elmer, will you check out the back rooms?" I asked. "See if anything looks unusual."

"Yes, I'd be glad to." Elmer patted my shoulder. "You just relax a little, Ivy," he said, trying to placate me. "Everything will be okay."

As he toddled off, I hissed at Amos. "What is wrong with you? You're the one who told me to be careful. Then when I'm actually attacked, you act like I've lost my marbles."

He knelt down next to my chair. "Listen, Ivy, I believe you thought someone was here, but the truth is . . ." He took a deep breath and brushed a strand of hair from my face. "The truth is, you ran into the front door and knocked yourself out."

"What? Are you nuts?" I was incensed. How could he think I would do something so stupid?

"Look, I'll show you." He stood up and walked over to the front door, which was made of thick glass. He patted a spiderweb-shaped crack that was right about where my forehead would be if I was standing up — or galloping full speed into an immovable object.

Even though I was still a little woozy, I pulled myself up to my feet. "But that's impossible. I hit the bar on the door with both hands. It should have opened."

"Under normal circumstances, it would have," Amos said patiently. "But there's a dead bolt on the metal doorframe." He pointed to a knob I hadn't noticed before. "Elmer locked it when he left. When you went galloping toward the door, you hit the push bar with both hands, but the dead bolt kept the door from swinging open. You crashed headfirst into the glass." He shook his head, his face creased with concern. "The truth is, you probably got off lucky. If the glass had broken . . ."

I sank back down into the chair and set my chin in my hand. "Okay, I get it. But, Amos, there *was* someone here. Maybe I caused my own headache, but I really did hear loud noises coming from down the hall. That's why I ran."

His expression made it clear that he was

having a hard time believing me.

"I'm telling you the truth," I said, glaring at him. "Someone was in this building. I called out, thinking it was Elmer, but no one answered. Right before I hit my head, I heard someone call my name."

Amos started to say something but was interrupted by Elmer's return. The diminutive funeral director looked embarrassed. His eyes darted back and forth between me and Amos.

"Well, I checked out the building," he said hesitantly. "Everything seems in order."

"But I heard a loud crash," I said. "Like something metal falling to the floor."

Elmer shook his head, his face registering his pity for my mental state. "I do have some aluminum trays stacked in the embalming room," he said kindly, "but they seem to be all right, although I will have to speak to Billy Mumfree about them. I've told him a hundred times about not putting the trays directly on top of each other."

"But what about the phone?" I could hear the defensiveness in my tone, and I hated it. I recognized the voice of the old Ivy, the insecure girl who'd had no control over her own life. Angrily, I pushed her away.

Elmer stared at his shoes for a moment before answering. "I'm sorry, Ivy. I know this isn't what you want to hear, but you accidentally kicked the phone cord out of the wall jack for the phone line. It's located right next to the desk, under the jack for the computer line. The connection is loose. I do it all the time. I should have warned you about it. I'm sorry."

I wanted to defend myself, but I was tired and my head hurt like the blazes. I grabbed the arms of the chair and forced myself up again. Amos reached out to steady me, but I pushed his hand away. "I need to get my stuff out of the office," I said to no one in particular. "Then I'm going back to the bookstore to get some sleep."

"You stay here," Elmer said. "I'll get your things."

I wanted to protest, but I really wasn't sure if I could make it down the hallway without falling over.

"I've got my car out front," Amos said gently. "I'll drive you back and make sure you've got everything you need."

There wasn't anything I wanted from Amos right then, but I had no choice. There was no way I could walk all the way back to the bookstore.

Elmer came trotting down the hall with my stuff. "Let me carry these out to the car for you," he said, indicating the inventory books and my notebook.

I thanked him while Amos took my coat and helped me into it. Elmer followed behind us while Amos held on to me until we got to the car. Once I was inside and my things were in the backseat, I waved good-bye to Elmer as he stood in front of the funeral home, looking dejected. I tried to smile at him, hoping to lift his spirits a little, but it didn't seem to help much. Elmer Buskin wasn't used to being happy, so the unfortunate circumstance fit his already gloomy view of life.

"I'm going to call Dr. Barber. She needs to take a look at that bump on your head," Amos said as we pulled out into the street.

"It's nothing. It might look bad for a few days, but the swelling will go down. The only thing wrong with me is this whale of a headache. A few aspirin should take care of it." The story of how I ran into a door while being chased by an invisible intruder wasn't something I wanted dispersed throughout town.

"Ivy Towers, I'm not asking you this time. I'm telling you," Amos said harshly. "What if you have a concussion? You can't take the chance."

"I think I can decide for myself whether or not I want to see a doctor," I replied, choking back a rush of unwelcome emotion. "I am not some weak-minded little numskull who needs to be taken care of by you or anyone else."

I didn't want to cry in front of Amos, but I didn't seem to have a choice. I wasn't even certain why I was weeping. Was it a release of the fear I'd felt in the mortuary? Or was it the hurt caused by Amos's lack of trust in my version of what had happened? Probably a little of both.

Amos pulled the car over to the side of the road. "Ivy, I'm not trying to tell you what to do. I'm trying to help you." His words were clipped with irritation. "Why are you so defensive? Why am I suddenly the enemy?" He turned around and stared out the windshield. His hands were clenched on the steering wheel while his jaw tried to work out his frustration.

I wanted to say something, but I was too upset. I felt alone. My parents were overseas, Bitty was gone, and the one person I really trusted in Winter Break didn't believe me when I needed him most.

Finally, Amos started the car and drove me back to Bitty's. He helped me inside and got me settled on the couch in the sitting room. After running upstairs to get some aspirin and a glass of water, he covered me with a quilt and started a fire in the fireplace.

"Look, Amos," I said, trying to calm him, "I'm sorry I upset you. You're not my enemy, but back at Elmer's you certainly didn't feel like my friend. A friend believes you when you tell him something."

He sat down next to me on the stone hearth and cradled his head in his hands. When he looked up, his expression was composed. "Okay, Ivy. Even though it doesn't make sense, I believe you. I'm sorry I let you down." He ran one hand through his sandy hair. "I try hard to look at things with an eye toward the facts. You're asking me to take what you say on faith. I guess I need practice." He grinned at me. "I know you think being a deputy sheriff who lives in Winter Break doesn't take much effort, but you'd be surprised. This town has had its share of problems. This isn't the first time something unusual has happened here. I guess I slid into lawman mode back at the mortuary."

The look on my face made him laugh. "Believe it or not, last year a couple of big-time bank robbers holed up outside of town thinking no one would pay any attention to them here. And the year before that, I uncovered a group stealing cars and bringing them to Winter Break to strip and sell parts. There was a murder in Hugoton six months ago. Right now, the sheriff's office in Stevens County is searching for someone who killed a spouse for the inheritance money. Law enforcement in Minnesota think the killer might be hiding out somewhere in the area." He shook his head. "It isn't all store-bought jam and stolen cows, Ivy. I've been involved in a lot of important cases."

I shot him an amused look. "Yet Hiram Ledbetter seems to slip away time after time. I guess it's because he's got such a devious criminal mind."

Amos glowered at me. "Hiram Ledbetter is a lot smarter than you give him credit for. As long as he's selling *liniment,* he's not doing anything wrong. I'll catch him someday. You can count on that."

"I think Sherlock Holmes said the same thing about Dr. Moriarty," I said innocently. "I didn't realize you were also locked into a battle of wits against an evil archenemy."

His expression made me giggle. That sent a shot of pain all the way through to the back of my head. I winced.

"I don't like this at all," Amos said. "I'm going to call Lucy and tell her what's going on. I'm not sure you should wait until tomorrow to see someone."

"For crying out loud, Amos. I told you I was okay. Don't bother the doctor." To be honest, even though I didn't want him to call Lucy Barber, I was more focused on his use of the doctor's first name. This was the second time he'd called her Lucy. I was starting to wonder if he and Dr. Barber had more than a doctor-patient relationship.

Amos ignored me, just as I knew he would, and went into the bookstore to use the phone. Even though he wasn't all that far away, I couldn't make out what he was saying. After a few minutes, he put the phone down and came back.

"Lucy seems to think you'll be okay. You haven't thrown up and you don't seem confused . . . well, at least not any more than usual."

I stuck my tongue out at him. "Very amusing. I told you I was okay. If I felt something was seriously wrong, I'd tell you. I'm not a martyr."

"She told me to ask you if you were having any problems with your vision."

"No," I said, stifling a yawn. "It's good enough to see that it's getting late, and you need to go home. I'm pretty tired."

"Okay, I can take a hint."

"Not very well," I mumbled.

"Dr. Barber will be here in the morning to check on you," he said, ignoring me. "And before you get all huffy on me, she was coming for the funeral anyway. I'll feel better knowing she's checked on you."

Miss Skiffins, who had just come into the room, jumped up on the couch and nestled down on my chest. "Well, that kind of settles that," I said. "I guess I'll spend the night on the couch."

"Maybe I should stay here, Ivy. How do you know that the person at the mortuary won't come here? I could sleep in one of these chairs."

I shook my head. "This place is locked tight. I'll be fine. If I hear any strange noises, I'll call you right away. I promise."

Although I meant what I said, I knew that Amos still had doubts about my stalker. If he'd really believed me, he would have insisted on staying without giving it a second thought. His hesitance made me want him to leave. I had some things to think about, and I couldn't do it with him here.

"Okay. I'll call you in the morning to check on you," he said. "What time?"

"No earlier than eight."

"One last thing," Amos said, crouching down next to the couch. "Please forgive me

194

for not believing you, okay?"

"No problem."

He patted me on the arm and left, making sure to lock the door behind him. I knew I hadn't been honest with him. There was a problem. A big problem. I was now convinced that I needed to get out of Winter Break as soon as possible. I was becoming someone I didn't want to be. Someone I'd been trying not to be for a long time. It wasn't just Amos's lack of faith in me; it was more than that. It was my lack of faith in myself. I was beginning to understand that somehow, Winter Break was changing me in a way I couldn't accept.

Even though I had many conflicting thoughts rolling around inside my achy head, I made the firm decision to sell out to Noel Spivey based on my best guess as to the value of Bitty's books. That seemed to be the fastest way to get out of this one-horse town. But first, Amos and I would figure out what really happened to my great-aunt. Nothing was going to make me leave before that was accomplished.

As I lay on Bitty's couch, with the fire sputtering in the fireplace, I felt something heavy pressing down on my chest. It wasn't Miss Skiffins, who was purring with contentment. It was something else. Something

I couldn't define and didn't want to.

And whatever it was frightened me a lot more than being chased in the dark through Buskin's Funeral Home.

11

I woke up around seven the next morning,
feeling a little bit better. A quick check in
the bathroom mirror showed the swelling
had gone down. At least I was beginning to
lose the look of someone who should have
her own tent in the circus sideshow. However, the spot where I'd made contact with
Elmer's door was now turning a lovely
shade of dark purple. My only hope was to
cover it with makeup. I rummaged around
in Bitty's cosmetic bag and found some
heavy foundation and powder. With a little
luck and some creative hair styling, maybe
no one would notice my colorful lump. I
had no desire to answer questions that
would force me to recount my late-night
escapade at Buskin's.

I was already on my second cup of coffee
when Amos called at eight o'clock on the
dot. After assuring him I was fine and accepting a ride to the church, I headed for

the shower. The hot water felt good on my shoulders. They were tight — a sure sign of tension. I stood under the nozzle for a while, thinking about the decision I'd made the night before. I was certain it was the right one. It made sense in my head. School was waiting. One more semester, and I'd have my degree. Even more important to me right now, I could go back to being the person I'd been before coming here. Samantha was beginning to feel like a long-lost relative who'd moved away, and I had every intention of finding her, and myself, again. I was starting to realize that I hadn't really lost Ivy Towers. She was alive and residing in Winter Break. If I didn't get out of here soon, I could become her again. I couldn't allow that to happen.

One obstacle I faced had to do with the money I'd make from the sale of Aunt Bitty's inventory. What would I do with it? How could I profit from her death and probable murder? Yet I knew she wanted me to have her inheritance. Perhaps I'd pay off my student loans then give a chunk of it to Faith Community. Maybe the church could even use the building that housed the bookstore. I wasn't certain what they could do with it, but if I gave it to them, all I would have to do was sign over the deed.

After I took what I wanted from Bitty's possessions and fulfilled her personal bequests, the rest of her property could also be donated to the church. Her friends could each take something to remember her by, and the church could sell the rest.

With all these thoughts running through my mind, I stepped out of the shower and dried off. Then I pulled on my bathrobe and wrapped the towel around my head. I was on the way to find something to wear, when I heard a noise from downstairs. I went to the top of the stairs and looked down. Someone was at the door. I wasn't excited about the idea of greeting a visitor in my bathrobe, but there wasn't time to get dressed first. I ran downstairs and opened the door a crack, trying to peek around the side so that whoever was standing out there wouldn't see my ratty terry cloth robe.

A young woman bundled up in a parka, snow boots, and gloves stood on the porch with a black bag in her hand. "Ms. Towers?" she said. "I'm Lucy Barber. Amos Parker asked me to drop by and take a look at the bump on your head."

I hesitated a moment, feeling at a disadvantage without my clothes.

She smiled. "I see you've just gotten out of the shower. If you'll let me in, I'll be glad to wait while you get dressed."

Not seeing any way out of it, I opened the door. "Yes, please do come in. I'm sorry. It will just take me a minute to throw some clothes on."

Dr. Barber stepped inside, stomping the snow off her boots and onto the floor mat. "From what Amos said, I'm sure you're fine, but it never hurts to be absolutely certain."

I stood there clutching my threadbare robe while I watched her remove her coat and gloves. Lucy Barber was a strikingly beautiful woman with long, ebony hair and eyes the color of dark chocolate. I could see a hint of Indian heritage in her flawless features. She was tall, with a lithe body that would be the envy of any aerobics instructor.

I felt short, dumpy, and wet. "Have a seat, Dr. Barber," I said. "I'll be right back."

She smiled at me. "No problem. Take your time."

Without any hesitation, she started toward the sitting room. I was learning that this was par for the course in Winter Break. I wondered if there were any townspeople who *hadn't* spent time in Aunt Bitty's bookstore.

After pulling on some jeans and a shirt

and trying to do something with my wet ringlets, I dragged my bruised noggin, along with my more severely bruised ego, into the sitting room. I felt like a soggy, slightly disfigured gnome in the presence of this natural beauty. My poor self-image shook hands with some kind of sour sludge lodged in the pit of my stomach. I knew exactly what it was — jealousy. The thing I couldn't understand was *why*. I wasn't in love with Amos Parker. What did I care if he wanted to hang out with Miss America in a doctor's uniform? It wasn't any skin off my nose.

"Why don't you sit down?" Dr. Barber said. "I want to get a good look at your injury."

I dutifully complied, allowing her to poke and prod my battered forehead. She took a small penlight from her bag and shined it in my eyes.

"How do you feel this morning?" she asked after nearly blinding me. "Any blurred vision, headache, or upset stomach?"

"No, no, and no," I said, trying to blink away the big white spots that danced before my eyes. "I had a really rotten headache right after the accident, but I took some aspirin and I feel okay now."

She jabbed my forehead once again.

"Of course, it is still a little tender," I said

with tears in my eyes.

"Oh, sorry," she said. "You're fine, but you are going to have a lovely bruise for a week or so. However, I don't see any evidence of concussion." She dropped her little light back inside her bag. "If the headache comes back, or if you have any unusual symptoms, give me a call."

"Okay. Thanks."

As she turned to leave, I stopped her. "Dr. Barber, I wonder if I could ask you a few questions about my aunt's accident."

I realize that after being bonked on the head, things may seem a little fuzzy for a while, but I was perceptive enough to see a drastic change wash over Lucy Barber's face. It was as if someone had suddenly turned out the light and closed the door. Her compassionate doctor expression disappeared, and something akin to wary suspicion took its place.

"There's really nothing I can tell you," she said, still moving toward the door.

"Please. I know you saw her right after she . . . after she fell. I'm her niece. Surely you can spare a few minutes."

Her reluctance was obvious, but she came back and sat down across from me. "What is it you want to know?"

"I'd like to hear why she died. What did

you see when you got here?" I had a few other questions, but I decided to ease into them. The good doctor reminded me of a cornered animal. If I moved too fast, she'd probably run away.

With a sigh of resignation, she put her bag down on the floor and leaned back into her chair. "When I arrived, your aunt was already gone. She'd fallen off the ladder, striking her head on the bottom roller cover. There was serious blunt force trauma to the right side and significant bleeding — internally and externally. The fall most likely caused an immediate lack of consciousness, followed by death." She frowned at me. "I could go into details about what happened inside her skull, but you wouldn't understand it. I don't believe she suffered."

"Did you try CPR?"

Once again, that invisible door slammed shut in my face. "She was gone, Ms. Towers. Her brain was irreparably damaged. No amount of CPR could have brought her back."

I wondered about her ability to see into my aunt's head without X-ray equipment, but I choked down my skepticism. "You ruled the death an accident and had Elmer pick up the body?"

She nodded. "That's right. I believe your

aunt had already taken care of her final arrangements with Mr. Buskin. I saw no reason to interfere with those wishes."

Frankly, I was beginning to find the doctor's smugness a little irritating. I don't care how gorgeous she was, I didn't like the cavalier way she had disposed of Aunt Bitty. My attitude led to my next question, which, in retrospect, I should have phrased a little differently.

"Dr. Barber, did it ever occur to you that someone else might have caused my aunt's death? Shouldn't you have at least considered the possibility and asked for an autopsy?"

Her expression turned stormy. "Are you accusing me of something, Ms. Towers? If so, why don't you just come out with it?"

I swallowed the angry bile I felt bubble up from my chest into my throat. "I'm not accusing anyone of anything . . . yet. I just find it strange that my aunt's body was sent out and cremated before anyone had a chance to find out what actually happened. Maybe things are done that way in Winter Break, but I don't believe most health-care professionals would handle a situation like this in a similar fashion."

Dr. Barber sprang up from her chair and glared at me, her dark eyes flashing. "Now you look here. Your aunt was my friend. I cared deeply for her. If I could have saved her, I would have. You're talking about things you know nothing about. Perhaps if you'd bothered to show up once in a while, you'd know better than to sling accusations at her friends. I doubt seriously if Bitty would appreciate your actions. The only person around here who should feel guilty is you!"

She stomped her way out of the sitting room and grabbed her outer clothing from the coatrack. I followed behind her, too angry to speak. Just who did this woman think she was? She'd never had the kind of relationship I'd had with Bitty. I knew that under my ire ran a strong undercurrent of guilt. I *should* have been here. That knowledge made me more irate. "I'm not finished with this," I warned her. "I intend to find the truth about my Aunt Bitty — either with you or without you."

Dr. Barber whirled around and pointed her finger at me. "You need to be careful," she said in a low voice. "Trying to blame the wrong person for Bitty's death just might land you in big trouble."

She pulled on her coat, jammed her feet into her boots, and flung the door open. Aunt Bitty's bell jangled with alarm. I watched as she tromped out to her silver SUV, shooting one last fierce look toward the bookstore. As she pulled away, I realized I was shaking. Her last words sounded like a threat. My intuition told me that Dr. Lucy Barber was hiding something, and I intended to find out what it was.

I was dressed and ready by twelve thirty when Amos pulled up outside. Rather than make him come in, I opened the door and motioned to him to wait in his car.

Although the bitter temperatures had kept the snow from melting, the sun was actually shining. It was the first time since I'd arrived in Winter Break that the sky hadn't been overcast. Maybe God had lifted the clouds out of respect for Bitty. He would have a tougher time breaking apart the dark animosity hanging over my heart.

When I had myself belted in, I looked up to find Amos staring strangely at me. "What?" I asked. "Is something wrong?" I reached up to pat my hair, making sure it wasn't out of place any more than normal. I looked down and checked the black dress I hadn't worn in years. I'd originally bought it five years ago for the funeral of a friend of my father's. But it wasn't faded, and thankfully, the hem wasn't stuck in my pantyhose.

"I . . . It's nothing," Amos said.

He looked a little flushed. Not unusual in this kind of cold, but odd for him. "Are you sure you're okay?"

He nodded. "You look nice, that's all. I'd forgotten how well you clean up."

"Oh, thanks. I must look pretty awful under normal circumstances."

He started to put the car in gear. I reached over and touched him. "Wait a minute, Amos. I need to talk to you before we get to the church."

I quickly recounted my odd meeting with Dr. Barber, finishing with her last comment. "I think she was threatening me, Amos. I'm convinced she knows something she's not telling us. I don't trust her."

"That's ridiculous, Ivy. I know Lucy very well. She cares a lot for all of her patients. She was particularly close to your aunt. You implied that she didn't do everything she could for Bitty. I don't blame her for getting upset."

"Listen," I said, "Dr. Barber was in town the day Bitty died, remember? She was at Ruby's, although we have no idea just when she got there. She could have easily gone to the bookstore before she went to the restaurant."

He shook his head and put the car into

gear. "No way. You don't know Lucy."

"And you do?" I could hear the resentment dripping from my words, but I didn't care. "Seems like you and the hot doctor are pretty close. No chance that's coloring your perception some, is there?"

Amos shifted back into PARK and scowled at me. "Why would my relationship with Lucy be any of your business? You have no right to ask any questions about anyone in Winter Break. You've made it crystal clear that there's nothing here you care about. You see yourself as some strong, sophisticated person named Sam who's too good for us small-town hicks. You hate it here so much you've tried to rid yourself of the person who used to care about this place and the people who live here."

For a moment, I was struck dumb by the emotion behind his words. "Amos, I didn't mean it to sound like that," I said, finally finding my voice. "My decision to distance myself from Ivy has nothing to do with Winter Break. It's me." I could feel tears trying to make an entrance, but I forced them back. I leaned over and laid my head on his shoulder. "It's me," I said again. I stared out the front windshield, searching for the right words. "I . . . I've spent most of my life feeling like I don't belong any-

208

where. My parents are such self-assured people. They've always known what they were called to do. To be honest, I've just been someone in the way. A problem that had to be 'dealt with.' "

Amos started to say something, but I hushed him. "Let me finish."

He nodded and closed his mouth.

"Coming to Winter Break was, I don't know . . . different. I felt like I belonged here. But when I went home, I was still Ivy, living in my parents' shadow." I could feel a tear force its way out of the corner of my eye. I dabbed at it quickly with the side of my hand. I didn't want black streaks of mascara decorating a face that was already disfigured. "When I started college, I decided to change who I was and become the person I wanted to be." I pulled away and turned my head to look at him. "That's why I changed my name. It was a fresh start, a chance to find out what kind of person I really am. Without my parents, without feeling that I had to live up to anyone else's expectations. Winter Break was never the problem, Amos. The truth is, I love it here. But I can't go back to being Ivy. I can't pick up all that insecurity and fear again. I just can't."

Amos was silent for a moment. Then he

reached over and brushed a stray curl from my face. "My beautiful Ivy," he said gently. "Have you ever considered that instead of deserting the person you used to be, you should allow God to heal her?" He shook his head. "Leaving her lost and confused doesn't sound right to me. She doesn't deserve it." He touched my cheek once again. "I know you think you can leave her behind, but I don't believe we can ever be free from our hurts without first giving them to God. Feelings buried alive never die, Ivy. No matter how deep you bury them."

He put the car into gear and pulled out into the street. We rode the rest of the way to church in silence. His words rolled over and over in my head. Was he right? Had I tried to cover up my problems instead of dealing with them? As we drove into the parking lot, I forced myself to put my questions aside for now. It was time to say goodbye to Bitty.

Amos unbuckled his seat belt and started to reach for the door handle.

"Wait a minute," I said. "Before we go in . . ." I tried to muster up a smile, although I wasn't feeling particularly cheerful. "I will think about what you said, but I want you to respond in kind."

"What do you mean?"

"I want you to honestly consider what I said about Lucy Barber. Quit coloring her with your own emotions. You told me you like to look at the facts. I think the evidence is compelling. She was in town. She was the one who pronounced Bitty dead, and she sent her to be cremated without an autopsy and without allowing anyone else to view the body. And she is definitely hiding something. Her reaction to me was way over the top."

He sighed. "What do you want me to do?"

"Nothing right now. But we need to add her to our list of suspects."

He grunted. "So far our list of suspects pretty much includes the whole town."

"I know it seems that way, but until we can find a reason to rule someone out, we can't afford to ignore anyone."

He sighed again, but at least this time he accompanied it with a small smile. "Hope my name doesn't end up scribbled in under Lucy's. You've never asked me where I was the morning of her death."

"I never suspected you," I said with a grin. "You still feel guilty about stealing strawberry pop from Dewey."

He shook his head. "You know, every time you tell that story, you leave out one very important thing."

"And that would be?" I said in my most innocent voice.

"You forget just who was waiting outside the Food-a-Rama for that second bottle."

"I have no idea what you're talking about. I think growing older has dulled your memory."

"Well," he said, looking down at his watch, "at least I can still tell time. We'd better get in there. It would be a little embarrassing for you to be late to your own aunt's funeral."

As we entered the church, I was amazed by the number of people jamming the lobby and filing into the sanctuary. It was standing room only.

When Elmer saw me, he hustled Amos and me into the pastor's office and closed the door. "We'll wait until everyone else is in place, then you'll enter and take your seat," he said. "Would you escort her, Deputy?"

Amos nodded. "I'd be happy to if it's okay with you, Ivy."

"Yes, that would be fine." I was grateful to have someone's arm to hold on to. Butterflies were beating their wings wildly inside my stomach. I wasn't sure why. I had no reason to be nervous, yet I was. I reminded myself that today was about Bitty, not me. That helped a little.

Elmer left the room, returning a few minutes later. He motioned for us to follow him. I took Amos's arm and we exited into the lobby. I could hear the strains of one of Bitty's favorite hymns being played on the organ. I could almost hear her singing: "Softly and tenderly Jesus is calling. . . ."

Elmer waved us on, and Amos and I began our long walk down the aisle to the front row. I snuck a look at some of the people waiting to bid Bitty farewell. I spotted Dewey, who gave me an encouraging smile. Lila Hatcher sobbed into her handkerchief. Lucy Barber refused to look my way, and Ruby Bird waved at me, her flaxen wig topped with a black netted pillbox hat. Although it was a style more popular in the sixties, I was touched that she had tried to tone down her audacious hairpiece. I saw Isaac sitting next to Alma Pettibone. He glanced up at me as we passed. I was startled by the grief etched into his face. I looked around for Noel. I didn't want to stare, but I thought I saw the back of his head over to the side in the fourth row.

After we sat down, the organist finished her song. Then Pastor Taylor came up to the podium. On a table in front of the stage sat Bitty's final resting place. The Bible urn was surrounded by pictures of my great-aunt. Behind the table was an easel that held a large picture of her smiling face. It was a posed shot, like something you'd see in a church directory. Bitty looked lovely. Her silver hair still had streaks of auburn. It curled softly around a face that expressed a joy that only knowing God's love could explain. The twinkle in her eyes seemed to be there just for me. I couldn't tear myself away from them. They were mirrors of the love and compassion that dwelt in the depths of Bitty's soul. Although in my mind I already knew she was dwelling in the presence of the One she loved the most, staring into those eyes confirmed it beyond a shadow of a doubt. She had always lived with her gaze focused toward heaven; taking up residence there had simply been the next natural step for her.

I opened my purse and pulled out one of the tissues I'd wisely jammed inside before leaving the bookstore. I was surprised when Amos held out his hand for one, too. I reached for another, noticing that his eyes were as teary as my own.

Pastor Taylor came up to the podium, and we all turned our attention toward him. "We are gathered together here today," he began, "to say good-bye to a friend. Although she

214

is on a journey that will separate us for only a short while, we will still miss Bitty Flanagan. I'd venture to say that there isn't one man, woman, or child in Winter Break who isn't affected by her passing or who wasn't touched by her life."

The thought flashed through my mind that there was at least one person who wouldn't miss her. I could feel Amos glance over at me. I was pretty sure he was thinking the same thing.

"I used a word a moment ago," Pastor Taylor continued, "that epitomizes Bitty Flanagan. The word was *friend.* Bitty was a very spiritual woman, but also very human. Although I would be hard-pressed to think of any weaknesses she ever expressed, I can easily tell you one of the strengths she possessed. I can tell you the one characteristic she exhibited more perfectly than anyone I've ever known. That quality was friendship. Bitty knew how to be a friend. John 15:12–13 says, 'My command is this: Love each other as I have loved you. Greater love has no one than this, that he lay down his life for his friends.' Bitty laid her life down every day for all of us. There wasn't anything she wasn't willing to do. There wasn't anyone she wasn't willing to love." He glanced around the room. In that moment of silence, I could hear the sound of weeping. It was coming from everywhere. I realized that Amos himself was almost overcome by emotion.

An odd feeling came over me as I realized that Bitty Flanagan hadn't thrown her life away in Winter Break the way my mother had said. She'd shared it. She had impacted the lives of people in a way I could barely understand. And even though I knew today wasn't about me, I couldn't help but wonder about my own funeral someday. Would this many people come? Would they feel the kind of loss these people felt? Would they grieve this way about me?

I tried to listen to Pastor Taylor, but my mind wouldn't focus. Comparisons between my life and Bitty's kept filling my thoughts, no matter how hard I tried to push them away.

After speaking for a while, Pastor Taylor stepped away from the lectern, and a young woman walked up to the microphone. The organist began the moving strains of "What a Friend We Have in Jesus," and the girl began to sing. Perhaps we were all sitting in the small town of Winter Break, Kansas — a place most people in the world had never heard of — but I couldn't imagine that anyone, anywhere, at any time, could have sung that song more beautifully. The whole church seemed to catch its breath and hold it until the final notes faded away.

I was surprised to find tears streaming down my face. I'd forgotten all about my mascara. I started dabbing as quickly as I could, hoping it wasn't too late.

Then Pastor Taylor came back to the microphone. "We have some people who have asked to say a few words about Bitty."

He stepped back, and one by one, the citizens of Winter Break expressed their love for my aunt. Between sobs, Lila Hatcher talked about coming to Winter Break as a widow, feeling alone and abandoned. But then my aunt became her friend and gave her a reason to live, getting her involved in church and even sharing her love of books. Dewey Tater talked about the years he cared for his dying mother and the way Bitty was always there to brighten up both of their spirits. The way she spent hours reading to the elderly woman so Dewey could get some much-needed rest. He credited my aunt with teaching him about love.

One by one the people came, pouring out their hearts. It was one of the most moving things I'd ever seen or experienced.

Then Odie Rimrucker came to the front, his cheeks wet. "Bitty Flanagan saved my life," he said in a deep, rumbling voice. "Pure and simple."

He glanced around the room as if he thought he might find Bitty sitting somewhere, listening. He cleared his throat and stared down at the pulpit for a moment. I thought I saw his lips move. When he looked up again, he was a little more composed.

"I know most of you people remember when I was a drinker," he said slowly. "In fact, I was a drunk. It don't matter what it was that first drove me to drink. We all have our problems. I expect most of us have some deep sadness in our lives somewhere. For whatever reasons, I never felt like I belonged anywhere. I never felt like anyone wanted me. I thought I was just a mistake that God let slip through somehow. I was so pained on the inside that I drank, trying to make the hurt go away." He wiped his eyes with the back of his hand. "But drinkin' don't help nothin'. Drinkin' only makes it worse. 'Course, I couldn't see it back then." He smiled a little. "I thank all you people who tried to help me, especially Deputy Sheriff Watson. He never gave up on me. I sure wish he was still with us. I really do miss him." He nodded toward Mrs. Watson and her two sons, who sat a few rows from the front. "So many people tried to help me, but for some reason, none of it took. It wasn't that any of you did anything wrong. You didn't. I just couldn't listen 'cause my mind was locked up with sadness. Then one day, my beautiful wife left me and took my children. That was the end for me. I decided to drink myself away. I drank so much I thought I would go to sleep and never wake up. That's what I wanted to do, but Bitty Flanagan had another plan, and no one could stop her when she set her mind to somethin'."

A twittering of laughter swept through the room. Bitty's stubbornness was well known. I couldn't help smiling at the memory of her jutting out her jaw, pointing her finger at whomever happened to be handy and saying, "If the devil thinks he's going to make me back down, he's got another *think* coming."

I turned my attention back to Odie, who was busy battling emotions that threatened to overtake him. His mouth trembled as he spoke. "Bitty had the deputy take me to her place to sleep it off. She took care of me for several days. When I finally woke up, stinkin' of booze and vomit, she cleaned me up and poured coffee down my throat, even though I wanted nothin' of it."

Odie's rotund face flushed at the unflattering image he'd portrayed of himself. I could only imagine the strength it took for him to face the person he'd once been.

"It weren't that Bitty told me much different than anyone else had, 'bout how I needed to change my ways and let God heal me, but she did somethin' no one else had ever done."

Odie tried to choke back the tears and regain control of his unsteady voice. He quit looking at the crowd and focused on something in the back of the sanctuary — something only he could see. "Bitty Flanagan didn't just tell me what I could be. She told me who I already was. She saw somethin' good in me even then. She didn't see no dirty stinkin' bum. She saw the Odie down deep inside, the one who hurt and wanted to be loved, and she loved *him.* I didn't think no one could do that. Leastwise me. She showed me that God Almighty knew the truth about old Odie Rimrucker. And that He loved me jes' the way I was." He shook his head slowly. "I almost couldn't believe it," he said. "But I knowed Bitty Flanagan weren't no liar. And if she said God loved me, it must be the truth. She showed me what God's love really is. Love that comes to you no matter what a low-down, dirty dog you are. Love that accepts you just as you are but also believes in what you are gonna be someday. And when you know God sees you like that, well, you know you can really be somethin' different. When you finally believe you're not just a failure, a little light goes on inside that starts givin' you the strength to be somethin' else."

He looked over at me. "Miss Ivy, as you is the only living relative here at this service, I want to thank you for your aunt, Miss Bitty Flanagan. I'm here today, sober and in church, 'cause this great lady helped me to reach out and find God's love. I'm purely grateful. All I can do to honor her is to try to be the person she knew I could be. Thank you."

Odie walked away from the pulpit to the sounds of clapping. I wondered if there were very many funerals where people actually broke out in applause. But today, at the funeral of Miss Bitty Flanagan, it certainly felt right.

After a few more testimonies, we all sang two more hymns that Bitty loved. Then the service was dismissed.

Elmer came to the front of the church and directed Amos and me to the lobby. I stood there for a long while, accepting hugs and words of appreciation about Bitty. I finally saw Noel. He came up and put his arms around me, promising to call me the next day so we could talk more about the bookstore. I could barely contain the warmth that filled me at his embrace. Amos ignored him completely, turning to talk to someone else so he wouldn't have to face him.

Through a break in the crowd, I saw Isaac leaving through a side door. He stopped for a moment and looked my way. I got the feeling he wanted to say something to me, but seeing the long line of people, he gave up and walked out. It didn't matter. We were definitely going to have a conversation — and soon.

Lucy Barber also left without speaking to me, but I saw her wave at Amos. He looked her way and smiled, but he didn't wave back. Probably because he knew I was watching him.

Just when I thought everyone was about gone, Ruby Bird came flying up toward me, yelling, "My poor, poor Ivy." I couldn't help but wonder if someday, someone was going to suggest she get a hearing aid. It seemed as though she got louder every day. "Your aunt was a dear, dear friend," she hollered. "In fact, she was one of the few people I trusted in this whole world." Then crazy Ruby Bird whispered something in my ear. Well, let's say she softly shouted it. "Your aunt is the only person I ever shared my secret with," she said with a note of triumph. "She knew everything that goes into a Redbird Burger." She glanced around the almost empty room as if she really believed no one else could hear her. "And if you play your cards right, honey, I'll tell you, too, someday."

The weight of her pillbox hat was pulling her ridiculous wig over to the side of her head, making me worry that the whole thing was about to fall off, exposing what was underneath. I was pretty sure I didn't want to know. Her poor scalp hadn't seen the light of day for at least twenty years.

"Thank you, Ruby. That means so much to me. Will I see you over at Lila's?"

Also sensing the possibility of an imminent wig disaster, Amos put his hand on my back and began moving me toward the front entrance.

"Land sakes, child," Ruby bellowed, "I plumb forgot. I've got to get over to the restaurant and get the food for the open house." When she hugged me, I wanted to reach up and pull her wig back to where it was supposed to be. I forced myself to keep my hands down. "I'll see you over there," she said. Then she galloped out the front door.

Pastor Taylor watched the whole escapade. After Ruby disappeared down the steps, he broke out in giggles. I don't know if it was a release of tension or something else, but Amos and I both joined in. Finally, after we stopped laughing, Pastor Taylor wiped his eyes and shook his head. "My goodness," he said. "Ruby Bird is certain proof that God has a sense of humor." He smiled at me. "You'd better be careful, young lady. The story about Bitty knowing Ruby's secret ingredient will be all over town by the end of the day. And if she ever really tells it to you, that will be your last peaceful moment in Winter Break."

We said our good-byes, and I thanked him for the beautiful service. Amos and I went outside and got into the car.

It took only a few minutes to get to Lila's. I loved the old Biddle place. It was built in the early 1900s by a man named Silas Merryweather. Mr. Merryweather had it in his mind to change Winter Break from a stopping point on the way west to a large, thriving city. He'd come from the East Coast, bringing lots of money and even more ambition. After building his Queen Anne–styled Victorian home, he began trying to lure other businesspeople to town. Unfortunately, after experiencing the long, harsh winters that seemed to plague Winter Break, the brave businesspeople who had ventured out west to catch the next wave of prosperity went away broken and bankrupt. Merryweather's ship never came in, and eventually he gave up and left town. Since then, many families had lived in the lovely old home with its turrets and balconies. Before the Biddles, the home had fallen into disrepair, but Cecil Biddle had worked hard to bring it back to its original splendor.

Funny how I compared all homes to this grand old structure. In my imagination, whenever I thought about having my own family someday, I saw us living in the Biddle house. Having never really lived in a place that felt like home, I found this house had become the standard, the home of my dreams.

We turned the last corner, and the Biddle homestead loomed up in front of us. Its backyard faced Lake Winter Break. The Biddles had been the guardians of the lake in the winter. Cecil would check the surface every day, and when it was finally frozen hard, he would raise a little yellow flag he'd attached to a pole in his backyard. When the flag was up, the town's children knew it was okay to venture out with their skates. Marion would make hot chocolate in a big thermos and bring it to us. I could still taste it. It was the best hot chocolate I'd ever had.

"Ivy, are you okay?" Amos asked after parking the car. "You seem a million miles away."

"I was remembering all the good times we had here. I'd forgotten about so many of them." I reached over and squeezed his arm. "Sorry. I'm ready. Let's go in."

Lila's house was packed with people. A few minutes after we arrived, Ruby poked her head in and yelled for some "big, strong men" to help her unload her truck. Lila's long banquet table was soon loaded with enough food to feed the entire town for several days. Although I wasn't hungry, I followed Amos through the line, taking small samples from the spread laid out in honor of Aunt Bitty.

Besides the food Ruby brought, there were all kinds of goodies carried in by other townspeople. The Baumgartners were out in force, so there were bowls of sauerkraut and apples, red cabbage, and potato dumplings. Someone brought a tray of bratwurst, and on the dessert table, amid Ruby's scrumptious pies, sat decorated stollen loaves, Black Forest cake, apple strudel, and my favorite, baklava.

Hannah Blevins, a longtime friend of

Bitty's, donated her famous apple-and-green-tomato relish, made from a recipe that had won several prizes at the state fair. Alma Pettibone, the postmistress, brought her wonderful huckleberry jelly and home-made huckleberry muffins. Every summer, she visited her sister in Oregon, and they would put up jars and jars of preserves. Alma always brought back a huge batch of jelly, along with extra huckleberries for baking. She passed out the wonderful jelly to many of her customers in Winter Break. Of course, Aunt Bitty always got several jars. She and I would bake bread together, and when it cooled enough, we would slather huckleberry jelly on it. That jelly was a little bit of heaven in a jar.

I grabbed a couple of Alma's huckleberry muffins and a spoonful of jelly and went searching for butter. It was in the middle of the table, shaped into the image of a graceful swan. The mold used to shape the butter was very familiar. It was Bitty's, passed down from my great-grandmother and, according to Bitty, eventually destined for me.

"What's wrong?" Amos whispered. "You're holding up the line."

As I reached for some butter, someone came up behind me and gently touched my back. I turned around to see Lila standing there with tears in her red-rimmed eyes. "I suppose you recognize your aunt's butter mold?"

I nodded.

"Your aunt gave that to me because I loved it so," she said softly. "I think you should take it back, though. It should stay in your family." Lila reached into the pocket of her dress and took out a hankie. "She was too generous," she said, wiping her brimming eyes. "I'll wrap it up and give it to you to take home."

"No, Lila. If she gave it to you, you should keep it. You must have meant a great deal to her. I know how much she treasured that mold."

I finished taking everything I wanted and began looking for a place to sit down. Lila took my elbow and guided me toward a couple of empty chairs. She sat down next to me and leaned in close.

"Your aunt was the best friend I ever had," she said. "We were like two peas in a pod. We both lived similar lives, you see. Although she lost Robert when she was young, and I lost my Milton when I was in my fifties, we both understood grief. I can't tell you how much Bitty's friendship meant to me. She had a way of filling up all the empty places with hope." She dabbed at her eyes again. "I swear, I don't know what I'm going to do without her. I feel so alone."

Trying to balance my plate on my lap, I reached over and patted her hand. "There are many, many wonderful people in Winter Break," I said. "You won't be lonely. And the church has lots of activities. They'll keep you busy."

Her fingers trembled as she touched her salt-and-pepper curls. "Yes, that's true. But it's not the same as having someone in your life you can tell everything to." Her smile was thin and forced. "I'm sure you don't understand that. Being so young and beautiful, you must have lots of friends. But for someone my age . . . well, people like Bitty just don't come along every day."

I wanted to comfort her, but she was right. Bitty was special. She would be impossible to replace. "Lila," I said, "if Bitty hadn't considered you family, she never would have given you that mold. I'm sure she felt just as strongly about you."

The older woman broke down and sobbed into her hankie. "I don't know what to say," she whispered after she composed herself. "I hope it consoles you a little to know that Bitty had many, many friends. I know her last days were happy ones."

"Believe me," I said. "I'm beginning to realize that she was a very blessed woman."

Lila nodded. "That she was, dear. That she was." She stood up. "I hope you'll stay in Winter Break. We could be such good friends. I feel it in my bones."

My bones weren't planning to stay in Winter Break, but I smiled at her anyway and nodded. As she walked away, her words came back to me. *"Someone in your life you can tell everything to."* It did sound wonderful. There was no one in my life now with whom I felt that comfortable. As kids, Amos and I were pretty close. We'd shared almost everything. Emily Baumgartner had also been a good friend. Correction: Emily *Taylor.* I looked through the crowd, but I didn't see her.

I was enjoying my second muffin, when Alma sidled up next to me. "I remembered how much you always loved my jelly and my huckleberry muffins. I made that batch of muffins just for you."

"Thank you, Alma," I mumbled, my mouth full but extremely happy. "They're just as good as I remember."

"May I sit down?" she asked, motioning to the empty chair next to me.

I swallowed and wiped my mouth. "Of course, please do."

Alma Pettibone was a woman who was

passionate about two things: her soaps and town gossip. She was a kindhearted woman, but her tongue had gotten her in trouble more than once. Bitty used to warn me that telling something to Alma was just like standing in the middle of Main Street with a bullhorn and announcing your business to everyone within earshot. I think she really tried to curb herself, but she was weak. It occurred to me that maybe I could take advantage of her shortcoming. The post office was right across the street from the bookstore. Alma had a clear view of everyone who came and went. It was possible she saw something that could point me in the right direction. I silently chided myself for not thinking of it sooner.

"Alma," I said quietly, looking around to make certain no one else could hear us, "the morning that Bitty died, did you happen to notice who visited her?"

She scrunched up her face and looked at the ceiling. I wasn't certain what that meant, but I surmised that she was trying to remember. "Hmm. Now that was last Wednesday, wasn't it? That was the day that Marla Mason told Dr. Naismith that his wife had been seen in the company of that nasty Brock Davis."

She stopped looking up and flashed me a

triumphant smile. My blank expression must have given her a clue that I had absolutely no idea what she was talking about. She cupped her hand around her mouth and whispered conspiratorially, "I watch *As Our Lives Turn* at ten o'clock every weekday, and I sit right in front of the window. I can see everything that goes on outside."

She had obviously found a way to combine her two favorite things. I was impressed. "Did you notice anyone visiting the bookstore during the time your program was on?"

"I certainly did!" she exclaimed. "Of course, earlier that morning, Dewey went over for breakfast. He did that every morning. Then Isaac came in for work. That was before my programs started."

"I specifically want to know who went to the bookstore between ten and eleven o'clock."

Alma clucked her tongue several times. "My goodness, dear. I understand, but I'm not one of those computer machines. I can't just push out information when you press a button." Her silver topknot jiggled in frustration.

"I'm sorry, Alma," I said in an appropriately apologetic tone. "Please go on."

"Well, let me see. Oh yes. Your aunt had a couple of visitors that morning after Isaac picked up the packages from the post office." She wrinkled up her nose again. "That snooty Dr. Barber came by."

I found that information interesting. "Do you remember how long she was there?"

Alma shook her head. "No, I'm sorry. I had to make a trip to the little girl's room. I didn't see her leave."

I glanced around again, but no one was paying any attention to us. "Alma, why do you call Dr. Barber 'snooty'?"

She raised her eyebrows and pursed her mouth. "That woman had the nerve to tell me that if I'd turn off the TV and give my eyes a rest once in a while, I wouldn't get so many headaches."

I was fairly certain Dr. Barber's diagnosis was right on the money, but this wasn't the time to antagonize Alma. "You said someone else stopped by?"

The old woman nodded so vigorously, her bun looked like it was caught up in some kind of frantic dance routine. "Before the doctor stopped by, Dewey Tater went running back to the bookstore. This was a couple of hours after he'd left earlier that morning." The sparkle in her eyes showed that she was warming up to the gossip that had been thrown into her already-willing lap. "I thought that was kind of unusual. Dewey usually never leaves his store once it's opened. He looked like he was upset about something."

Her words were like ice water thrown into my face. "Can you be more specific about the time?"

"Well, if I remember right, Dr. Naismith had just started operating on Angela Marstairs." She sighed and shook her head. "That girl just never learns. I mean, she wouldn't have needed that operation to relieve the pressure on her brain if she hadn't been snooping around in things that shouldn't concern her." Alma leaned closer. I could feel her breath on my face. "You know, she is really June Anne's mother, but —"

"Alma," I said, trying to keep a note of hysteria out of my voice, "the time Dewey went to the bookstore?"

Her hand went to her chest. "Oh yes. I almost forgot." She screwed up her face again. "Why, it would have been right around ten fifteen. My show hadn't been on that long, and the operation was before the second commercial break. I'm sure of it."

"Thank you, Alma. Was there anyone else

you can think of?"

She looked at me sadly. "Well, Isaac came back a little while later. Then Dr. Barber and Dewey. By then, our dear Bitty was gone." A tear crept down her face. "I know I go on and on about my soaps, dear. Bitty used to scold me about them sometimes. But she understood."

"She understood what, Alma?"

Winter Break's postmistress hung her head. When she spoke, I had to strain to hear her. "She understood that my soaps keep me from feeling alone. They keep my mind off my troubles." Her brown eyes sought mine. "Your aunt told me that I needed to get out and spend more time with people, but I'm terribly shy. I promised her I'd try someday — when I was ready. She believed me, Ivy. Even though I didn't mean a word of it."

"I'm sure she did, Alma," I said. "By any chance, did you see anyone else?"

She shook her head. "No, that's all I can remember."

"And did you leave your chair any other time except for that bathroom break?"

"No, that was it." Alma stared down at the floor for a moment. "Wait a minute. That was Wednesday. April Tooley comes in every Wednesday at ten thirty to mail a package to Marvin. He's in the army, stationed overseas. She won't set her package on the counter like everyone else does. She makes me process it right then and there." Alma's face flushed a little, and she lowered her voice to a whisper. "She says I forget things sometimes. I humor her because her brother is over there risking his life for our freedom."

"And about how long does it take to get her package ready to mail?"

"Oh, I don't know. I'd say it takes me about ten minutes. We like to gab a little. 'Course, I end up missing some of my program, but it's the least I can do for one of our men in uniform."

Her smile showed her pride in doing her part for our country. I wasn't sure that missing ten minutes of a soap opera once a week was that much of a sacrifice, but who's to say? Maybe to Alma it was a real gift from the heart. I thanked her for the information, and she wandered away, probably looking for a television somewhere.

As soon as she left, Amos edged up next to me. "We need to talk," he said in a low voice. "I've dug up some interesting dirt."

I grinned at him. "Are you trying to tell me that you're pumping people for information at my aunt's memorial service?"

He wrinkled his nose at me. "Oh, and you were in deep conversation with Alma Pettibone so you could catch up on the soaps?"

"Okay, you got me. I have something to tell you, too. I think we're going to have to wait, though, Amos. I can't leave now."

"But this is important."

His obvious frustration fueled my interest. I glanced around the room. "Let's go sit by the fireplace; no one is there."

I stood up and ambled slowly toward one of the chairs near the brick hearth on the other side of the room. Most of the guests were near the buffet table. As long as they hovered near the food, Amos and I would have some privacy.

I stopped first at the kitchen and dumped my plate into a trash container. Then I continued my slow walk toward the fireplace, hoping no one was watching me. Amos followed nonchalantly. I had a notion that we probably looked highly suspicious, but when I scanned the room, it appeared that no one had noticed us. They were too busy eating and talking.

"Okay, who goes first?" Amos asked after we were seated.

"Age before beauty," I said.

"Thanks a lot," Amos said. "But I'll take it." He glanced around us once more then scooted closer so no one could hear him. "First of all, Morris Dinwiddie told me he was coming back Sunday night from Hiram Ledbetter's farm after buying some 'medicine.' "

"So what? How does that help us?"

He sighed and shook his head. "If you'll just hush a minute and listen, you'll find out."

"Okay. Don't get snarky."

His eyebrows shot up. "*Snarky?* Is that one of those big-city words?"

I rolled my eyes. "Sorry. Don't get all het up. Is that easier for you to understand?"

"I'm not a hundred years old," he grumbled.

I was getting exasperated. "Are you going to tell me what you heard in this lifetime, or should I just plan on spending the rest of my existence in this chair waiting for you to get around to it?"

He mumbled something else that I refused to acknowledge. "Morris Dinwiddie saw Isaac skulking around in the dark near Buskin's right around the time you knocked yourself out."

I grabbed the arm of my chair. "What?"

Amos swung his head around to see if anyone had noticed my rather loud exclamation. "Shh. You heard me." He put his hand on my arm. "Ivy, I think he was coming from the mortuary."

"I told you there was someone there. He was following me."

He held up his hand like a traffic cop. "Now wait a minute. He may have been in the building, but let's remember that he didn't actually hurt you. You ran into that door all on your own."

"Maybe I beat him to it," I hissed. "You have no idea what his intention was."

"Well, you certainly were an easy target, lying on the floor all passed out. If he'd wanted to do something to you, why didn't he use the opportunity you so brilliantly provided him?"

I didn't have an answer for that.

"The point is," Amos said softly, "it was probably Isaac in the building that night. That's what you heard. We need to figure out what he was doing there."

I started to say something, but Amos hushed me. "That's not all. Here's something else interesting. Your friend Noel has been placing and receiving a lot of calls at Sarah's."

"He's a book dealer, Amos. Of course he gets a lot of calls."

Amos leaned back a little, and I could see he was definitely pleased with himself.

"Okay, give. What are you so happy about?"

"Almost all the calls are from one person."

I was growing weary of this cat-and-mouse game. "All right, I'll bite. Who were the calls from?"

"Someone named . . . Olivia."

I had to admit, I hadn't seen that one coming. "Olivia? Our Olivia?"

He shrugged. "I don't know, but I think the coincidence is intriguing at the very least."

I sat back in my chair to think for a moment. Noel was a book dealer from Denver. What could he have to do with the shipment of books sitting in the bookstore? And who was Olivia?

"I think we should try to find the Olivia who sent those books," I said. "It may be important."

"But you said the labels from the boxes were missing, and there weren't any references to any Olivia in Bitty's books."

"What about Alma? Doesn't she have to keep some kind of records?"

"I don't know," he said. "But we'll definitely ask. As far as Noel Spivey as a suspect," he said, looking skeptical, "you know I'm not crazy about the guy, but this doesn't really make much sense. He doesn't even live here; in fact, he said this was the first time he'd ever been in Winter Break."

"Even so, we have to check out every lead. Frankly, the idea of someone who didn't know Bitty killing her makes more sense than someone who did." Even as I said it, I couldn't believe it. Noel Spivey didn't seem like a killer to me.

"Now tell me what you found out," Amos said.

I informed him about Bitty's extra visitors on the day she died.

His eyebrows shot up at the mention of Lucy Barber, but he didn't say anything. However, he immediately dismissed the idea that Dewey was hiding something.

"But Alma said he looked upset," I said. "I think that's significant."

He grunted. "First of all, Alma has a flair for the dramatic. She probably confused one of her soap opera actors with Dewey. I'm telling you that Dewey had nothing to do with Bitty's death."

I started to say something about Amos believing in Dewey because he cut him slack for stealing that strawberry pop, but I was interrupted by Pastor Taylor, who suddenly came up behind us.

"This is a nice turnout, isn't it?" he said, gazing around the crowded room.

"Bitty would have been honored," I agreed.

"I hope you know how much she meant to us. I will really miss her, sitting in church and smiling at me during the service." He chuckled. "You might not believe this, but the other side of the pulpit can be rather disconcerting. Sometimes during your most rousing sermon, you're greeted with yawns and glassy-eyed stares. And that doesn't include the people who are trying to look as if they're reading their Bibles but are actually sound asleep." He sighed deeply. "But Bitty was always bright-eyed and interested. And always looked happy to be in church. Yes, I'm really going to miss that," he said again.

I started to stand, but Pastor Taylor waved me back down. "Please don't get up. I'm sure you're tired. It's been a long day. I didn't want to bother you, but I thought I might stir the fire a little. These old houses are hard to keep warm, and some of the guests are getting a little chilly."

He walked around to the hearth and grabbed some tongs hanging from a tool rack. After he turned the logs over a couple of times, the fire crackled back to life. Watching him reminded me that we still needed to buy tongs for Bitty's fireplace. I mentioned it to Amos.

"Don't know where you can get any fireplace tools in Winter Break," Pastor Taylor said. "We had to go to Hugoton for ours. I think some people order them through the mail. 'Course, you have to pay shipping that way." He put the implement back on the rack. "I see Lila has some extra tools. She'd probably give you whatever you need."

I shook my head. "That's not necessary. We're doing fine." I didn't want to say out loud that it didn't matter that much since I wouldn't be staying long enough to worry about it.

Pastor Taylor sat down on the brick hearth. "I hope you weren't offended about the cash memorials to the church. I wouldn't have brought it up if Bitty hadn't mentioned it to me."

"I'm sure it's exactly what she would have wanted. I have to say that I was touched by all the flowers that showed up anyway. People in Winter Break are very generous."

"I don't know that it was generosity. I think it was more gratefulness than anything else." His eyes misted. "Bitty touched a lot of people in her life, Ivy. More than you realize, I think." He wiped his eyes and smiled at me. "I hope you'll be around for a while. I believe Bitty left you a wonderful legacy.

I'd like to see you get blessed by it."

I nodded but kept my mouth shut. I was beginning to understand that leaving Winter Break was going to be a lot tougher than I had ever imagined.

As Pastor Taylor walked away, Amos said in a low voice, "We need to get out of here. We've got a lot to talk about. I also think I figured out another entry on Bitty's list."

I started to remind him that this reception was for me and that I couldn't leave early when Dewey came up and put his hand on my shoulder. "Doing okay?" he asked.

"I'm fine, Dewey. How about you?"

He walked over and gazed into the fire. "I'm feeling the loss a little more today than I did yesterday," he said. "Don't know why. But I keep reminding myself that God's family is eternal. Even when we're apart, we're still together." He looked at me and smiled sadly. "You probably think that's silly."

"Actually, I don't. I miss Bitty, but I can't shake the feeling that somehow, she's still here."

He nodded. "Yep. I feel it, too."

"It's almost like she has some kind of unfinished business, Dewey. Like she's trying to tell us something. Have any idea what that might be?"

Amos shot me a look of warning and cleared his throat. I ignored him.

Dewey's expression darkened. "I have no idea what you're talking about, Ivy Towers. I hope you're not spreading that ridiculous story about someone hurting Bitty. She wouldn't have stood for you doing something like that. She didn't believe in spiteful gossip."

I met his direct gaze without flinching. "I intend to do whatever I need to do to uncover the truth, Dewey. I think my aunt trusted someone she shouldn't have. I won't leave Winter Break until I find out who it is."

Dewey glared back and forth between Amos and me, his forehead knotted in frustration and his face slowly turning a nice shade of magenta. "Ivy Towers, I'm warning you. You'd better not stir things up that you can't fix, especially if you're not planning to stay around and clean up your mess." He stared at me for a moment longer then turned around and stomped off.

That was the second warning I'd received in one day. "See what I mean?" I hissed at Amos. "You keep telling me that Dewey couldn't possibly have anything to do with Bitty's death, but that isn't the way an innocent man acts."

"I don't think he's acting the least bit suspicious," Amos hissed back. "He loved your aunt and can't conceive of the idea that someone would purposely hurt her."

Amos cocked his head to the side, and my eyes followed his gesture. A group of people stood not far to our right. When they noticed us staring at them, they turned away. It was obvious they'd overhead Dewey's proclamation. I was a little embarrassed, but I was also somewhat relieved. Maybe if a few of Bitty's friends knew there was a reason to be suspicious about her death, we might uncover more information. I was certain Amos didn't share my feeling. I was right.

"I'm leaving," he said, standing up. "I think you've done enough damage here today. You can carry on without me."

"Amos, don't go. Please. I'm sorry." I tried to whisper, but my words came out louder than I intended. I didn't bother to look around. I was certain several of the guests overheard me.

He sat back down, but his mouth was tight with anger. "Ivy, I want you to ease back a little. I mean it. You don't know anything about handling an investigation. You need to trust me." His eyes snapped with emotion. "For crying out loud, this isn't rocket science. Blabbing everything we know right now could blow the entire case. We're going to shelve this discussion until we get back to the bookstore. In the meantime, I'm going to get a piece of Ruby's blackberry pie. Do you want anything?"

I shook my head. I'd kept him from abandoning me completely, but in truth, I was also a little peeved at his overbearing attitude. I cared a great deal for Dewey, but my main loyalty was to Bitty. Why was Amos so stubborn in his defense of almost everyone I suspected? At this rate, we'd never uncover the truth.

I was deep in thought when someone slipped into the chair Amos had vacated.

"Sam?"

Noel Spivey, cradling a coffee cup in his hands, looked incredibly yummy in an obviously expensive black suit. It draped his long, lean frame as if it were made specifically for him. It reminded me of a silk dress my mother had worn years ago. His eyes seemed to be an even deeper blue than before, and a lock of his wavy dark hair fell casually across his forehead.

The word *spiffy* crept into my brain. Spiffy Spivey. I bit my lip in an attempt to stop a giggle that threatened to make an inappropriate entrance. Then I remembered what Amos told me about the phone calls, and things didn't seem quite so humorous.

Perhaps it was Amos's condescending attitude, or perhaps it was just my own orneriness, but after I gave the debonair Noel my sweetest smile, I said, "Why, hello, Noel. Care to tell me who Olivia is?"

Maybe finding the truth isn't rocket science, but it doesn't take much more than a little common sense to know what it means when someone turns white as a sheet and spits a mouthful of coffee out all over you.

12

To say that Amos wasn't happy with me was an understatement. When he found me dripping with coffee and Noel trying to clean me up, he was quick enough to figure out that something noteworthy had happened. When I admitted to him that I'd brought up Noel's calls to Olivia, he ordered both of us back to the bookstore.

I made my excuses to Lila, thanking her for the lovely reception and promising to have lunch with her later in the week. Then Amos marched Noel and me out to his car and told us both to get in. No one said a word. When we arrived at the bookstore, Amos got out and pulled open the passenger door, along with the door to the backseat where Noel sat, and pointed toward the front entrance. We meekly followed his wordless instructions. My silence came from my fear that I had finally crossed the line with Amos. I couldn't ever remember him looking so angry. I had no idea why Noel was so quiet, but I suspected it was from guilt. The question was, guilt about what? Was he involved in a scam to get something valuable in Bitty's collection, or was he guilty of something much worse?

I was also beginning to worry that I had truly jumped the gun and given away something that might hurt us in our search for the truth. In my heart of hearts, I really didn't believe Noel Spivey was capable of murder. I couldn't find a motive. His only relationship with Bitty was through his long-distance business transactions with her. What possible reason would he have to come all the way to Winter Break, Kansas, to kill her? It didn't make sense. Besides, in this small town, someone would have spotted him and asked questions. New people never drift in and out of town without stirring up attention.

Amos herded us into the sitting room and pointed toward the two chairs that were immediately to meet our backsides. After we complied, he finally spoke. His first words were to Noel. He ignored me completely.

"All right, Spivey. I'm not thrilled that Ivy told you we know about your calls to Olivia, but that cow's left the barn. Now you're going to come clean. And don't try to tell me that your Olivia isn't the same one who sent two boxes of books to Bitty right before she died. There's no way that's a coincidence."

Noel didn't try to argue. Instead of responding to Amos, he addressed me. "Sam, there's one thing I want you to know before I tell you why I really came to Winter Break." Those striking eyes locked onto mine, and I found that I couldn't look away. I may not be the best judge of character, but I was pretty sure I saw sincerity there.

"I didn't tell you everything, but I didn't actually lie to you, either. I meant every word I said about how special I think you are. There's something about you that I find intriguing, and I don't want the truth to ruin any chance I have to get to know you better." He hung his head, and I could barely hear his next words. "I hope you'll give me a chance to explain, and I pray you'll understand."

To be honest, I was surprised by the intensity behind his words. I was also very aware that it sounded as if we had something much more involved going on besides a dinner and a kiss on the cheek. One look at Amos made it clear that he believed the worst. Or the best, depending on which side of the fence I was on. His expression could have been placed in the dictionary next to the explanation of what *looking daggers* actually means.

"If I were you, Spivey, I'd be more concerned about what *I* think about you," Amos hissed between clenched teeth. "Ivy can't lock you up."

Noel's head jerked up. "Lock me up?" he said, his face pale. "I haven't done anything illegal, Deputy."

"Noel," I said, "how did you find out that Bitty died? The only place it was published was in the Hugoton paper. You were in town before any of the other dealers knew about her death."

"There's a book buyer who lives in Dodge City. He gets the Hugoton paper. He saw it and called me."

Amos sat down on the fireplace hearth, next to the now visibly shaken man. "Okay, let's say we believe that. Now you need to tell us who Olivia is and why you're here."

Noel ran his hands through his carefully groomed hair, mussing it only slightly. "Olivia is my sister," he said quietly. "She sent those books to Bitty."

"I don't understand," I said. "You're a book dealer. Why wouldn't your sister work with you? Why was she involved with my aunt?"

He sighed. "She did it out of anger." His

fingers tightly gripped the arms of his chair. "You see, the books belong to our grandmother. She's been ill for the past several months, and Olivia has been caring for her alone. There are only the two of us to look after her. Our parents are both dead. Olivia asked me to come down and stay with Grams for a while so she could have a break." He shrugged. "I was too busy with my business, and I couldn't help her. She got upset with me and decided to cut me out of the situation. She found a nursing home for Grams and has been cleaning out her possessions."

"But if you didn't have time to help your sister, why are you here now?" Amos asked, his voice tight with hostility.

Noel shrugged. "I cleared my calendar, wrapped up all the deals I had, and went back to Cincinnati to help Olivia. I never told her I wouldn't help. I just wasn't able to come when she first asked me. By the time I got there, she'd already sent the books to Winter Break."

"But how did Olivia know about Bitty?" I asked. "She's not a book dealer, too, is she?"

He grunted. "No, Olivia doesn't know beans about rare books. She never wanted to learn anything about my business. She knew about Bitty because I'd told her about this place."

"That's very interesting," Amos said harshly. "But if she didn't care about what you did, why did you mention Bitty's bookstore to her?"

Noel smiled sadly. "Because I told her once that if I could do anything I wanted to do, I'd sell my lucrative business and open a bookstore just like this."

"But you told me that Bitty was running this place all wrong," I said.

"No, I told you that the way she ran it wasn't practical. I never said it was wrong." He gazed around the store, a faraway look in his eyes. "This is a magical place. There aren't many bookstores like this left, especially in small towns. What I wouldn't give to leave the rat race behind. . . ."

"Ivy said you made an offer for only the inventory, not the whole store," Amos said. "If you think this is such a great place, why didn't you offer to buy everything?"

Noel exhaled forcefully. "Because, old chap, I can't afford to move here and run a small bookstore. I could show Sam how to do it, but I have too many obligations to do it myself."

"Ivy," Amos said.

"Huh?" Noel stared at him in confusion.

"Ivy. Her name is Ivy. Quit calling her Sam."

I started to interrupt, but he glowered at me. I decided that in this case, discretion was the better part of valor. It seemed Noel also determined it was wise to mollify the man with the gun.

"Okay, sorry. Ivy, I mean."

"None of this explains why you came here, Noel," I said. "So your sister sold the books to my aunt. Why do you care? I've looked them over. There are some books there that are worth a few hundred dollars, but I couldn't find anything valuable enough for you to come all the way to Winter Break."

Noel straightened up in his chair. "You're absolutely right about that," he said. "But the book I'm looking for isn't in the boxes."

"What do you mean?" Amos asked.

"It's missing. There should be twenty-seven books altogether. There are only twenty-six."

"Noel, tell me about the missing book," I said. "What is it?"

"It's a first edition of Mark Twain's *The Prince and the Pauper*."

"How much is it worth?"

"Depending on the condition it's in, probably around fifteen hundred dollars," Noel said quietly. "I can't be more precise be-cause I haven't actually seen it."

"How much did your sister sell it for?" Amos asked.

"Five hundred dollars for the lot."

"Noel," I said, "I still don't understand. Were you really that upset about the deal? Did you come all the way to Winter Break because you felt cheated out of a thousand dollars?"

He shook his head slowly. "Olivia found that book right before she sent the rest to your aunt. She was trying to get rid of all of Grams's old books, so she tossed it in one of the boxes. The fact that the book was carefully wrapped up and kept in a trunk didn't get her attention. But it should have. If she'd ever tried to learn anything about my business, she would have realized that this book was different. She would have looked more carefully and discovered that there was something very special inside."

"I'm confused," I said. "You're looking for something *inside* the book?"

"Yes," Noel responded. He clasped his hands together and shook his head. "You see, Grams has Alzheimer's. She's had symptoms for many years now, but for the most part, it expressed itself as momentary lapses of memory. For as long as I can remember, she'd tell Olivia and me about some kind of 'treasure' she had, something she was saving for us. She never told us what it was. Then suddenly her disease took over. It crept up slowly and then pounced like some kind of wild animal, pushing Grams so far away from us, we couldn't find her anymore." He wiped his eyes with the back of his hand and cleared his throat.

"She seemed to lock on to 'her treasure,' asking us to find it for her," he continued, his voice shaky with emotion. "She tried to tell us about a book with a letter in it written to my sister." He shook his head. "It didn't make any sense. We brought her every book we could find, but she'd push them away. Then, after awhile, Grams quit mentioning it altogether. To be honest, my sister and I chalked it up to her imagination — and the disease that had so viciously attacked her."

"You never found anything that your grandmother might have seen as a valuable possession? Something she would want to pass down to you?" Amos asked.

"No. Of course, she had some antiques and a few rather valuable books, but nothing that explained her frantic attempts to get us to look for this so-called treasure."

"And then something changed?" I asked.

Noel nodded and straightened up. "Yes," he said with an air of resignation. "Something definitely changed. As I said, I went home as soon as I cleared my calendar. That's when I found out that Olivia had sent all of Grams's old books to your aunt." He shrugged. "I wasn't happy about it, but I wasn't that upset, either. I knew the books Grams had. Anyway, I thought I did, and although I think I could have gotten a little more for them, it wasn't enough to worry about.

"Olivia and I made up, and I started pitching in to help her get the house cleaned out while we made arrangements to put Grams into a very nice facility that specializes in Alzheimer's patients.

"Then one day, an old friend of hers stopped by. He'd known our grandmother and grandfather for many years. He even attended their wedding. Over coffee and doughnuts, he asked me what had happened to Grams's valuable book. Of course, I had no clue what he meant, and I told him so."

"Is there an end to this story at some point?" Amos asked impatiently.

I shushed him. "Go on, Noel. Just ignore him."

Noel took a deep breath, his eyes wandering toward Amos's gun. "That's okay," he said with a weak smile.

Amos glared at the both of us.

"Grams's friend told us that my grand-father had come across a first edition of *The Prince and the Pauper* that had originally belonged to Samuel Clemens . . . Mark Twain. Inside was a letter he wrote to his wife, telling her about his idea for a new novel." Noel's expression became wistful, and his voice softened as he became con-sumed with his story. "It was a story about a character he introduced in *The Adventures of Tom Sawyer*. One of Tom's friends . . ."

"Huckleberry Finn?" I asked breathlessly. "Are you saying that there was an actual letter from Mark Twain outlining his ideas for Huckleberry Finn?"

Noel stared at me for a few moments as if he didn't know who I was. Finally, he nod-ded. "Yes. And to top it off, it was written to his wife —"

"Olivia," I said. "His wife's name was Olivia."

"That explains why your grandmother kept connecting the letter to your sister," Amos said.

"Yes. If only I'd made the connection sooner."

"How much is it worth?" I asked. "I've seen old Twain letters in antique stores. I don't remember them selling for huge amounts of money. I believe he was quite a prolific letter writer."

Noel smiled. I think he forgot about Amos for a moment. His eyes sparkled with excitement. "Yes, that's true," he said. "The worth comes from who he wrote the letter to and the subject of the letter. This letter, if it really contains Twain's outline for *Huckleberry Finn,* would be a very valuable find. Another letter that expressed Twain's disgust with slavery recently sold for sixty thousand dollars."

"Sixty thousand dollars?" Amos said. "That's incredible."

"Yes. In fact, this letter could go as high as one hundred thousand dollars to a Twain collector."

Before I could say anything, Amos interrupted. "Sounds like enough money to encourage someone to commit murder." He stepped over and put his hand on Noel's shoulder. "I think we have our killer, Ivy."

Noel's eyes widened. "Now just a minute —"

"But Noel wasn't in town when Bitty died," I said, frowning at Amos. "Besides, why would he kill her? Why wouldn't he just break in and steal the book?"

"Because your aunt found out about the

letter," Amos snapped. "She knew how much it was worth and wouldn't give it up."

I stood up and faced Amos. "First of all, if my aunt had found a valuable letter that someone had accidentally sent her, she would return it. Bitty was unbelievably honest. And second of all —"

"You're right," he said bluntly, interrupting me, "but what if our friend Noel didn't know that? Maybe he didn't stop to ask questions."

"And second of all," I continued, "he wasn't in town, Amos. There's no way he could have killed Bitty from Denver."

Amos glared at Noel, who was keeping his eyes on Amos's right hand. I was afraid that if Amos moved toward his gun, Noel would soil one of Aunt Bitty's prized chairs. "And how do you know he didn't sneak out here, kill her, and then come back like he'd never been here before?"

Before I could respond, Noel timidly raised his hand. "If you two will give me a chance," he said, "I can prove to you that I was nowhere near Winter Break the day Bitty died."

"And how do you intend to do that?" Amos growled.

"Actually, I don't think it will be at all difficult," Noel said. "You said Bitty died on

Wednesday morning, correct? You see, I was being interviewed on live Denver television a little after ten thirty that day. KACL broadcasts a show called *Bookshop,* and I was the featured guest. It is physically impossible for me to be in two places at one time. It's a six-hour drive from Denver to Winter Break."

"Okay, okay," Amos said. "I get it. You couldn't have done it." He pointed a finger at Noel. "I'm going to check out your story. All I have to do is call the station."

Noel leaned back in his chair, much more relaxed than he'd been a short while ago. "Go right ahead, Deputy. You'll find I'm telling the truth."

I breathed a sigh of relief. I'd never believed that Noel was capable of murder. However, Amos looked rather disappointed. "Well," I said to my placated friend, "we know Noel couldn't have done it, and we also know something else very important."

Amos nodded. "We know why she was killed," he said. "Someone else found that book with the letter inside. Whoever it was knew how valuable it was and murdered Bitty for it."

"That's not all," I said. "We know that number eight on my aunt's list probably referred to Olivia. The murderer took the mailing labels, saw Olivia's name, and obviously suspected that Bitty was going to call *O,* the person who sent the books. Whoever did it was afraid that the missing volume would be discovered and that a search for the book would somehow lead to him. I think Bitty planned to call Olivia because there were more books in the boxes than there were supposed to be. She never saw the letter Olivia sent explaining the last-minute additions."

"That makes sense," Amos said. "Maybe that's the reason the list was taken."

I nodded. "Looks like it. Now we have to figure out who would have realized the value of a letter from Mark Twain."

He grunted. "We'd do better to figure out who *didn't* know. Anyone with half a brain would know it was worth something. I mean, we may be a little isolated in Winter Break, but we're not brain-dead."

"Yes, but not everyone in town was in the bookstore Wednesday morning. As far as we know, only three people were here," I said.

"What if someone came in the back way?" Amos asked, sighing. "Anyone could have come and gone undetected."

I went over to the door and checked the lock. The dead bolt wasn't turned, but the doorknob was locked. It would take a key to open it. Bitty used this door only during the summer when she tended her garden. In the winter, it was locked up and forgotten. There was no reason to go out that way. The trash cans were kept on the north side of the building and were easily accessible from the front entrance. Isaac's apartment was on the south side of the bookstore, and he had his own private entrance facing the street.

"Amos," I said, "did you check this door after you found Bitty?"

"As a matter of fact, I did," he said. "It was unlocked."

"And you didn't find that suspicious?" I asked. "I thought you knew everything about my aunt. Why didn't you know that she kept this door sealed tight during the winter?"

"Ivy," he said quietly, "your aunt has been buying large lots of firewood for the last couple of years. There was too much to keep in the inside log rack. She had a large outside cord rack installed next to the back door."

"I didn't know that. Sorry," I said. "I guess you really did know Bitty better than I did." I was ashamed to realize that I was a little jealous of how close Amos had been to Bitty.

"Ivy, it wasn't that I knew her *better* than

you. I didn't. No one was closer to her than you were. She just happened to tell me that she was becoming more sensitive to cold and wanted to keep stocked up with firewood. It's no big deal."

I pulled the door open. Sure enough, there was a large rack that contained several cords of wood. And there was something else. Something I'd forgotten. I closed the door slowly. "Amos, there are two doors that open up into the backyard," I said. "Bitty has one and Isaac has the other. That means that Isaac could easily have come in through the back door."

He shook his head. "That doesn't make sense. Isaac was seen by almost everyone on Wednesday. He was at the post office and the store. He went to Ruby's to pick up food. Why would he sneak in the back door when everyone already knew he'd been here?"

"What about the time lapse, Amos? The twenty minutes it took him to notify you? Maybe he snuck in through the back and —"

"Excuse me," Noel interrupted. "I know you two are busy being Nancy Drew and one of the Hardy Boys, but I wonder if we shouldn't check to see if my grandmother's book is somewhere else inside the bookstore. I looked through the boxes, but I've never had time to check out the shelves."

Amos raised an eyebrow. "That sounds logical. I don't think we're going to find it, but we might as well make certain."

An hour later, we finished checking the last row of books. We'd found two copies of *The Prince and the Pauper*. One was a first edition, in pretty good shape, but there wasn't anything written inside to confirm it had belonged to Noel's grandmother. We weren't really surprised when we opened the book and found there was no letter tucked inside. The other copy wasn't a first edition. It was a hardcover reprint from the sixties, not worth much to anyone except to readers like me. I remembered sitting on the front steps of the bookstore on a mild summer day, lost in the story of Tom Canty and Prince Edward.

Looking high and low through Aunt Bitty's books had forced us to use the rolling ladder. It was difficult for me to step up onto it the first time, knowing that Bitty's last moment of life occurred there, but it was strong and secure, and after a couple of times, my nervousness evaporated.

"Well, this was a waste of time," Amos said, standing up and dusting off his pants after perusing the final row of books.

"I'm sorry," Noel said. He held up the first edition we'd found. "This could be my grandmother's book, but I can't prove it. Since I never saw it, I can't identify it. Bitty could have easily had her own copy. I was hoping for a bookplate or a signature so I could identify it as Grams's."

"Maybe there is a way to tell," I said. "I'll go through her inventory books and check to see if there's an entry that refers to this book. It might take awhile. I have no idea when it came in."

"I wonder if I might be allowed to miss out on chapter two of your escapade," Noel said in a tired voice. "This has been a very draining day, and I'd like to crawl back into my feather bed at Sarah's for a late-afternoon nap."

"Okay," Amos said. "I'll take you to your car; then I'll come back. There's something else I want to talk to you about, Ivy."

Noel pushed himself up from the floor where he sat cross-legged. "I'll return tomorrow so we can talk about the books," he said. "At least all this searching has given me a pretty good idea of what's here." He came over to where I stood and took my hand in his. "I can't stay here more than three or four more days, Sam . . . er, Ivy. Olivia still needs my help."

I smiled at him. "I understand, Noel. We'll wrap everything up tomorrow, I promise. Why don't you come over after lunch — say around one?"

I walked Noel and Amos to the front of the store. Noel pulled on his coat then paused with his gloved hand on the door-knob. "There is one thing you should both consider as far as your thief and probable murderer. There is no easy way to sell this letter. It will be considered a very important find. By that I mean you can't just post it on eBay. Your killer must have some kind of plan to dispose of it. He's certainly not going to be able to get rid of it in Winter Break. In fact, he won't even be able to sell it in Kansas. He'll have to contact someone in a big city where something like this could be handled." He shook his head. "Even then it will be almost impossible to keep it quiet. If anyone claims to have 'found' it, collectors and appraisers will still want to find out where it came from."

"What if the seller can't give them what they want?" Amos asked. "Will that make the letter any less valuable?"

"Not really," Noel said. "The only really important thing value-wise will be its authenticity. If it was really written by Twain, that's all that's needed. However, a professional dealer will want to know its history so he doesn't end up with stolen property on his hands."

"So whoever has it will either have to bide his time or get out of Kansas." I shook my head and looked at Amos. "I hope we can catch this person without waiting around for him to try to skip town. Who knows how long that might take? I have to get back to school."

"You see if you can find that book listed in the inventory," Amos said, frowning at me. "I'll be back in a little while. After I drop Noel off at his car, I've got to run over to Maybelle Flattery's farm. She thinks Bubba Campbell's dog is eating her chickens. I promised I'd go by and talk to Bubba today. It shouldn't take long."

Noel paused again before walking out the door. "So there is actually someone living here whose name is Bubba?" he asked with a smirk.

Keeping a straight face, I replied, "Well, that's Bubba Campbell. There's also Bubba Johnson, Bubba Baumgartner, and way out on the north edge of town, there's Bubba Weber, who owns a honeybee farm."

My revelation wiped the smile right off his face.

Amos grinned and winked at me. "Come

on, city boy," he said to the disconcerted bookseller, "let's get you back to Sarah's."

I watched as Noel walked down the steps to Amos's patrol car, shaking his head. I closed the door behind them and locked it. After they drove away, I headed over to the desk to see if I could find any record of the Twain book.

I'd just unlocked the desk drawer and pulled out Bitty's most recent inventory book, when I heard a noise from somewhere near the sitting room. I'd barely gotten to my feet when in walked my number one suspect in Bitty's murder.

Isaac Holsapple stood at the entrance to the bookstore.

And he was holding a knife.

13

Okay, so in the right light a cake server kind of looks like a big knife. After being reassured more than once by an extremely mortified bookstore clerk that he had no intention of stabbing me — or serving me cake — I calmed down long enough to ask him why he'd snuck into the bookstore through the back door.

"I didn't sneak in, Miss Ivy," he said in his singsong, almost feminine-sounding voice. "I used that door all the time when Miss Bitty was . . . was alive." He cast his wide, dark, chocolate-colored eyes toward his feet. "I should have knocked, I'll grant you, but I just didn't think about it. Please accept my apologies."

"What do you want, Isaac?" I was wishing at that moment that Amos hadn't left. I didn't trust Isaac Holsapple, although I wasn't really afraid of him, either. He stood at only about five feet tall, so I had a good four inches on him. He was old and skinny and reminded me of an aging troll. I figured I could take him if it came to that. However, if he'd killed Bitty, he might have more going for him than met the eye.

He inched his way a little farther into the room. I had half a mind to tell him to stop where he was and drop his cake server, but I couldn't figure out how to say it without sounding like a really bad episode of some cop show. Not that I would know anything about that, of course.

"I . . . I wanted to return this," he said. "Miss Bitty lent it to me for the church dinner. I made a German chocolate cake and she gave it to me to use. It . . . it's yours now, of course."

Isaac's eyes kept darting around the room, almost as if he were afraid something was getting ready to jump out and attack him. He seemed so timid, so inconsequential, that in the light of day, the idea that he might be a murderer seemed rather ludicrous. But looks can be deceiving. He stopped a few feet from the desk and held out the silver server in his trembling hand.

"Just lay it down there on top of the shelf," I said, not wanting to get any closer to him than necessary.

He glanced at the small bookshelf next to

him that held a display of children's books. He looked so hesitant at setting something where it didn't belong, it was almost funny. Bitty had been an aficionado of "a place for everything and everything in its place." He was probably hearing her voice in his head. With much effort, he finally complied with my request.

"Well . . . thank you, Miss Ivy," he squeaked. He started to turn around to leave, but then he hesitated. He swung back around and fastened his huge eyes on me. "I . . . I want you to know how sorry I am about Miss Bitty's passing."

As I watched him, I realized that one of the reasons his eyes seemed so large was the strength of the lenses he wore in his round, tortoiseshell glasses. They not only magnified his eyes; they amplified his sadness. It was obvious he'd been crying. But had he shed tears because he missed Bitty or over regret for what he'd done?

"Thank you. I understand that you are the one who found her."

"Yes," he said. "I'd just come back from the restaurant. She . . . she was lying right over there." He pointed to the spot where Amos said he'd found my aunt.

"Isaac, I have to wonder why you haven't come to see me before today. I've been here since Friday night."

He retreated a couple of steps. "I didn't want to bother you, Miss Ivy. We don't really know each other very well, and to be honest, I'm a rather shy person. I would have said something to you at the service, but there were so many people around you."

I stood up and walked in front of the desk. "I understand," I said, leaning against the edge, "but what I really don't get is why someone would want to kill my aunt Bitty. Do you?"

I'm not sure just what kind of reaction I was looking for. Guilt, perhaps — or fear. But what I saw in Isaac's face wasn't either one. It was more like relief.

"No. No, I don't know who would want Miss Bitty dead," he replied. "She was a wonderful woman. Everyone loved her."

"I must say that you don't seem surprised by my question. Do you suspect that her death was something more than just an accident?"

He clasped his hands in front of him and stared at his locked fingers while he considered my question. "Miss Ivy," he said finally, his voice soft but firm, "I am convinced of it."

"You were the one who wrote that note on the envelope I left lying on the desk, weren't you, Isaac?" Why hadn't I seen it before? Isaac had keys to the bookstore. He was one of the few people who could have come in, even if I had locked the door that day. I'd been so busy suspecting him as the killer that I hadn't realized he was the obvious choice as the note writer.

He nodded with so much gusto, his long, stringy hair bounced around like frantic little worms trying to jump off his head.

"Were you in the funeral home Sunday night?"

"Yes," he said, lowering his eyes. "I've been trying to keep an eye on you. To protect you. Sunday night I followed you to the mortuary. It wasn't hard to get in. Billy Mumfree cleans the place on the weekends, but he never remembers to lock the back door. Unfortunately, I accidentally knocked some metal trays to the floor in the back room. Instead of keeping you safe, I frightened you. It's my fault you ran into the door and knocked yourself out." He raised his head a little. "I want you to know that I checked to see if you were badly hurt. I was going to get help when Deputy Parker showed up. I only left because I knew he would give you the assistance you needed. I'm very sorry about your injury."

I wasn't certain I believed him, but at least

his story explained why I'd had the uncomfortable feeling of being watched ever since I'd arrived in Winter Break. It also made it clear why the person stalking me inside Buskin's Funeral Home had left me lying on the floor instead of completing his attack.

"Okay," I said. "Now can you tell me why you believe someone killed my aunt?"

"I would be happy to," he said, "but perhaps we could sit down? My legs aren't as strong as they used to be. Sometimes they hurt me, especially when it's cold."

"All right." I followed him to the sitting room. He walked with a noticeable limp, and I wondered how old he actually was now. I'd never really thought much about Isaac as a person. He was more like a fixture in the bookstore. Like a clock or a lamp. Of course, that wasn't true. He was a human being, someone I'd never taken the time to get to know.

He gingerly lowered himself into the chair in front of the fireplace. I sat down in Bitty's rocking chair and waited for his explanation.

He cleared his throat a couple of times. "Miss Ivy," he said, "your aunt was quite adept on that ladder. If there was no other reason to think that something suspicious took place Wednesday morning, that fact alone should have caused questions."

"I agree," I said. "That was the first thing that made me wonder about her so-called accident."

"Then there were the footprints."

"Footprints? What footprints?"

"In the snow," he said slowly. "Usually, I am the only one who uses the back door, except when the weather is nice. I came in that morning after a fresh snowfall. But when I left for my apartment Wednesday, after Miss Bitty had been . . . removed, there were two sets of footprints."

"So whoever killed her left by the back way," I said, more to myself than to him. "When you say two sets of prints, Isaac, do you mean as if they had come and gone by the back door?"

"No," he said emphatically, "they used the backyard only once, when they left the bookstore. The footsteps only led away from the back door."

"Which means they came in the front door." I wasn't certain how helpful this information was, but it did show that whoever entered the bookstore that morning probably hadn't planned to kill Bitty. Something happened. Something that made this person feel the need to dispose of her. It also meant that someone might have seen the killer. The only people Alma mentioned were Dewey and Lucy Barber. I was suspicious of both of them. Alma's story about Dewey returning Wednesday morning, looking upset, concerned me. And Dr. Barber's stonewalling and defensive attitude certainly made her seem suspicious. Of course, it might not be either one. Alma had been away from her window for quite a while, helping April Tooley.

"There is something else," Isaac said, interrupting my thoughts. There was a note of triumph in his voice. "Something that no one else knows."

I raised my eyebrows as a sign to continue.

"Miss Bitty wasn't dead when I found her."

I almost jumped out of my rocking chair. "What? Dr. Barber told me she'd probably never regained consciousness."

He shook his head. "She was barely conscious when I found her. She only lived long enough to whisper two words to me."

"What did she say, Isaac?" I could hear the tremor in my voice. Aunt Bitty's last words. For some odd reason, I wanted to stop him from telling me. It made her final moments seem more real. Believing that she'd died instantly and hadn't known that someone she'd trusted had betrayed her had afforded me a measure of comfort. Now that was gone.

Isaac rubbed his hands up and down his skeletal legs. "I wonder if we could start the fire?"

"Yes, in a minute, but first I want to hear what my aunt said to you."

His owl eyes misted over. "She said . . . 'I forgive.' That's all she said, Miss Ivy. And then she was gone." A tear rolled down his wrinkled face.

The reality of Bitty's state of mind in the closing seconds of her life overwhelmed me. This was the death of a true Christian woman. Her last thoughts were of forgiveness. The revelation was almost more than I could bear.

"Why didn't you tell me this before now?" I asked when I could get the words out.

He shook his head. "I wanted to, but I was afraid you'd tell the wrong person. I didn't want to see Miss Bitty's killer leave town before you had a chance to catch him."

"But you wrote me a note, Isaac. What's the difference?"

"I believed that revealing my suspicions to you in this way would give you time to think it over and come to the correct conclusion. I counted on the fact that you would consider this to be a clue, as in the Nancy Drew books you used to read so much, and not just the crazy rantings of your aunt's rather odd book clerk." His slight smile told me that he was fully aware of how I saw him.

"I'm sorry, Isaac. I wish you would have trusted me enough to come to me immediately."

His smile grew and reached his mournful eyes. Funny how he didn't look quite so peculiar to me anymore. Actually, there was quite a bit of character in his face. I'd never noticed it before.

"That's okay, Miss Ivy. Now we have a long time to get to know each other."

I got a sick feeling in the pit of my stomach as I realized that Isaac thought I was going to stay in Winter Break and run the bookstore. This place provided him with more than a job; it was his life. What would he do when I left?

"Miss Ivy, if we're going to be working together, there's something else I think you should know. It . . . it's about me. Your aunt kept it a secret, and now I'm asking you to do the same."

My already-uncomfortable insides did another cartwheel. In my experience, the words *There is something I think you should know* really meant *I'm going to tell you something you'll wish I hadn't.* What was next? *I killed my mother and buried her in the backyard? My real name is D. B. Cooper? I like to dress up in a clown's costume and chase squirrels?* Then he said the last thing on earth I ever would have expected.

"Forty-five years ago, I caused an accident. That accident took the life of Robert Simmons, your great-aunt's fiancé."

There is a popular phrase that describes a condition of surprise that causes one's mouth to drop open. I discovered that it isn't just an expression. My jaw seemed to lower and hang at the end of my face all by itself. I was literally struck speechless.

Isaac removed his glasses and took a handkerchief from his vest pocket. He wiped his eyes. "I was drunk as a skunk the night it happened. I'd had a fight with my wife, so I went to the bar. I drank until I could barely stand up. Then I got behind the wheel." His voice got softer and more somber. "Back then, driving under the influence wasn't talked about like it is now. Still, I should have known better." He wiped his face again. "I never even saw Robert's car. I ran right into him. I wasn't really hurt — just a few cuts and bruises — but Robert was thrown from his vehicle and broke his neck. He died right there on the spot." Isaac cleared his throat, wiped off his glasses, and placed them back on his face. "As I said, in those days, drunk driving wasn't the bane of the road that it is today. I got off scot-free as far as the law was concerned. Not even a ticket. It was declared an accident. But I knew what I'd done — I'd cost that young man his life." Isaac shrugged and rubbed his thin legs again. "I lost my wife, my son, and myself that night. The guilt over what I'd done drove me to drink even more, until there was almost nothing left of me. I don't believe I would have lasted much longer, but your aunt heard about my condition and she came to me." He gazed at me with a look of something close to fondness, and I wondered if he was remembering Bitty when she was younger. I'd seen pictures of her around the time she opened the bookstore. She and I could have been twins. "She forgave me, Miss Ivy. She gave me a reason to believe there was hope for me, even giving me a job in her new bookstore. Little by little, I began to find my way back to life. I served her for over forty years, and every single moment was a privilege. She taught me that God loved me, no matter what mistakes I'd made, and that He was willing to give me another chance." His mouth quivered. "I owe her everything."

I was flabbergasted by Isaac's story. Forgiveness. Aunt Bitty had excelled in it, even forgiving the person who killed her. I suddenly felt very small and shallow. Not knowing exactly what to say, I got up to put some logs in the fireplace grate. I started the fire then reached for the canister that held the fireplace tools.

And I knew.

In that instant, everything came together. I knew who had killed Aunt Bitty.

14

I sent Isaac back to his apartment and began to check out several other things to see if they would support my conclusion. By the time I was thoroughly satisfied, Amos was back from Bubba Campbell's farm.

"Well, at least that case is solved," he said, stomping the snow off his boots and onto the floor mat. "Bubba's protests about his dog being unfairly blamed fell a little flat when old Barnabas came running up with a dead chicken in his mouth."

"Leave your coat on," I said before he unzipped his parka. "We've just solved another crime, and we're going to confront the perpetrator."

"What in blue blazes are you talking about?" he snorted. "What crime have we solved?"

As I pulled on my coat, I told him about my original suspicion, along with what I found during my research afterward. The skepticism in his face melted away as I explained.

"Well I'll be a monkey's uncle," he said when I finished. "It was there all the time. I should have picked up on it myself."

I grinned at him and opened the door. "It was elementary, my dear Watson."

"Okay, first of all, I'm not going to be Watson to your Sherlock," he grumbled, "and secondly, I thought you were an English major. You should know that Sherlock Holmes never even said that."

"Yes, I know that," I said, "but I'm surprised you do."

Amos tapped the top of my stocking-capped head with his finger. "We're not all a bunch of dumb yokels here, you know."

"I guess I do now, Deputy."

The joy of finally figuring out who had killed Bitty dissipated as we neared our destination. This wasn't just the end of a puzzle; we were getting ready to confront a killer, the person who had taken Bitty away from the people who loved her. I could feel anger bubbling inside me, but Bitty's last words kept playing over and over again in my mind, like the time the old McDonald's jingle got stuck there. *"You deserve a break today"* was replaced by *"I forgive, I forgive, I forgive . . ."* Unfortunately, I wasn't sure I was capable of being as loving as Bitty had been in her final moments.

About fifteen minutes later, Amos and I were sitting next to a crackling fire, being served tea and cookies. I put my cup down and stared at my aunt's murderer, who smiled at me as sweetly as she could. "So, Lila," I said, "how did it feel to kill your best friend?"

The blood drained from the woman's face, and her teacup slipped from her fingers, hitting the side of the coffee table and smashing to pieces. "Wha–what? What are you talking about?" she stuttered. She turned to Amos. "Deputy Parker, is this some kind of a sick joke?"

"No, Lila," he said gruffly, "this is definitely not a joke. I certainly don't feel like laughing."

Lila tried to pick up the pieces of her ruined china, but her hands shook so hard, she kept dropping them. Finally, she gave up. "I have no idea what you're talking about," she said, her pale blue eyes wide with fright. "You must be insane."

"I don't think so, Lila. You almost got away with it, didn't you? You know what finally tripped you up?"

I didn't actually expect an answer, and I didn't get one. "It was Aunt Bitty herself.

Her penchant for perfection: 'a place for everything and everything in its place.' "

"I'm sure I don't know what you mean," Lila said, her eyes shifting away from me and toward the door.

"I don't think I'd try it if I were you, Lila," I said. "I can guarantee you that Amos and I are faster than you. You'd never make it, and in the mood the deputy is in, I'm not sure what kind of force he would use to stop you."

That seemed to remove any thought of escape, but she wasn't admitting defeat yet. "There is no way in this world you can tie me to Bitty's death," she said. "Bitty fell. It was an accident."

"Actually, it wasn't that at all, and you know it. Would you like me to tell you exactly how it happened?"

Lila didn't answer. She still looked unconvinced, but I didn't expect her denial to last long. "Wednesday morning, you went to the bookstore to borrow my aunt's butter mold. You wanted to use it for the church dinner that night."

"Your aunt gave me that butter mold," Lila sputtered, "because we were such close friends."

"No, Lila. I should have known that story wasn't true. Bitty had already told me that she wanted me to have that mold. She never would have changed her mind without talking to me about it. That would have been going back on her word, and that was something she never did.

"You came over to borrow the butter mold," I continued. "My aunt probably went upstairs to get it. While she was up there, she put on some water for tea and put the tea bags in the cups. While she was gone, you noticed a shipment of new books, and being curious, you looked through them. You found a first edition of *The Prince and the Pauper.* You opened it and looked inside, making an incredible discovery. There was a letter written by Mark Twain to his wife, Olivia. You knew it was valuable, and you were convinced that my aunt didn't know anything about it since she had just opened the box and hadn't had time to go through it. You probably slipped the book and the letter into your purse thinking that you would be able to claim the book as your own, without anyone being suspicious. In the meantime, you might have glanced around for a packing slip — anything that might give a clue to the fact that the book with the letter was inside the box.

"Although you couldn't find anything like that, you did find a list on my aunt's desk.

Number eight on the list mentioned *O* and that there was a question about something *extra.* You knew from reading the mailing label on the outside of the box that the books had come from someone named Olivia. Obviously, my aunt intended to contact her about the shipment. You were afraid that if my aunt made that call, she would find out about the book. Even if the seller knew nothing about the letter, Bitty would know that someone had removed the book from the boxes. You'd never be able to explain how the book or the letter came into your possession without it pointing back to Bitty."

I paused for a moment. "That might have been the moment you decided to kill her. You needed to create a story that would be believed — a legitimate reason for you to have the book. I don't know when you put the book on the shelf, whether it was before or after you killed Bitty, but my guess is afterward. Just so you know, you put the book in the wrong place. My aunt never put books that were for sale with the books that were available for reading, yet I found two copies of *The Prince and the Pauper* on a shelf with regular books. The first edition didn't belong there."

Lila hadn't moved since I'd started talking, but she looked like a blow-up doll with a leak. With every new revelation, the wind went out of her a little more.

"After Bitty came downstairs, she either went up the ladder herself, or you sent her up for some reason. When she started down, you hit her on the side of the head with the fireplace tongs you'd removed from the canister."

Amos interrupted. "That's what Ivy meant about Bitty being the one who gave us the first clue," he said. "I'd complained about her lack of proper fireplace tongs. In fact, we were planning to buy some. Then, today, it hit Ivy. Bitty Flanagan would *never* be without the correct tool. Especially since she'd taken to using her fireplace so much. 'A place for everything and everything in its place.' Isaac confirmed for us today that he'd stirred the fire Wednesday morning and seen the tongs in the canister with the other tools." Amos stood up and walked over to Lila's tool rack. He reached behind the rack and held up a second set of tongs. They were brass, just like Bitty's set.

Lila ignored him and looked away with an air of resignation.

"You might have only knocked her out," I said, "but when she fell off the ladder and hit her head on the wheel cover, you were set. The original injury you caused was covered up by the massive wound that occurred because of her fall. You tried to position her in a way that made it look as if she'd gotten tangled up on one of the ladder rungs. Then you went looking for things that could point directly to you or to the missing book. You had to cover your tracks *and* end up with that letter in your possession."

"By then you'd realized you had no way of selling that letter," Amos said. "How would you say you found it? Would the letter tie you back to Bitty?"

"So you had an idea," I continued. "You removed the list from Bitty's pad so no one would know that you had been there or that Bitty had planned to contact Olivia. Then you took her keys and unlocked her desk drawer. You removed the page in the account book that mentioned the purchase from Olivia. You also knew about the list she'd made of things she wanted to leave her friends. You crossed off your name and added it again at the bottom. This time, you wrote in the first edition of *The Prince and the Pauper.* You put the book back on the shelf, knowing that someone would make sure you got it. That way, you could pretend to find the letter. You were fairly certain that even if I looked inside the book, I wouldn't check every page, so your claim of finding the letter wouldn't be challenged. Since you knew Bitty so well, you knew I would be the person in charge of her estate and that I probably wouldn't try to take that letter back. You were fairly confident you would be home free. The book was legally yours since my aunt had left it to you, and you could explain just how the book and the letter came into your possession. Since the original owner had sent Bitty the book, you assumed they didn't know anything about the letter. You hoped that any chance of connecting the book with that person was now gone."

Amos took the next part of the story. "You were lucky in some respects, Lila. You entered the bookstore while Alma was away from her window. Of course, after you killed Bitty, you couldn't take the chance that someone might see you, so you left by the back door. But you made some big mistakes. Isaac Holsapple saw your footprints in the snow. He knew someone had left the bookstore that morning by the back door. And you forgot that Bitty was making tea upstairs for the both of you."

"We were able to recreate a copy of the list Bitty made, Lila," I continued. "You were on it. Number four on the list was *BM for L — Don't forget!* Amos and I made a mistake when we read it. We thought the *L* was an *l*. Tracing over indentations from a missing piece of paper isn't an exact science. It loses something in the translation. Once I suspected you, I looked over the list again and realized that number four was a reminder that you would be picking up the butter mold to use for the church supper Wednesday night. That list was written Wednesday morning, Lila. That proves my aunt was expecting you. It also confirms that you *were* there because you have the butter mold. The only way you could have gotten it was to see my aunt on that very morning, sometime before she died."

Lila was staring at the floor. Finally, she said, "It all sounds very interesting, but can you prove a word of it?"

Amos gingerly carried the fireplace tongs in his gloved hand, being careful to stay away from the curved end. "If you're not convicted by all of the circumstantial evidence, Lila, I'm pretty sure this will be the final nail in your coffin. You may think you've removed all the evidence from it, but it's much harder to remove blood than you think. And there's no reason for you to have Bitty's tongs — unless you took them after you killed her."

"And of course, the letter is here somewhere, Lila," I said. "It will be found eventually."

"Yes, I suppose it will," Lila said. "I'll save you the trouble. It's in a box in my closet."

I was relieved to hear her confess, but at the same time, listening to her admit she'd killed Bitty filled me with intense anger.

"Lila, I have to ask you why you left the tongs lying out where they could be seen," Amos said. "Why didn't you dispose of them?"

Lila shook her head forlornly. "My goodness, Deputy, this is Winter Break. We have one trash hauler. That moron Maynard Sims thinks it's his business to check through everything I throw out. I can't tell you how many times he's come to my front door showing me something in my trash, asking if I really meant to throw it away." She sighed with exasperation. "I was afraid to throw out the tongs. Eventually, I decided to leave them near the fireplace since no one would think it odd." She stared at Amos with a look of disdain. "I'd been so clever at the bookstore, I thought I was safe. I hope this doesn't offend you, but you didn't seem sharp enough to figure out what I'd done." She swung her gaze at me. "But leave it to a relative of Bitty Flanagan's to refuse to let it go. If you'd just taken care of your aunt's business and left town, everything would have been all right."

It took every ounce of strength in my body not to jump off the couch and strangle her. Amos shot me a warning look.

"So what happens now?" Lila asked, smoothing her skirt. "I suppose you will arrest me, Deputy Parker."

"Yes, that's right," Amos said. "I'll take you to Hugoton and turn you over to them. There's a jail there. They'll take charge of you."

"I understand," she replied. "Ivy, I know this won't make any difference to you, but I want you to know that I didn't have any other choice. Bitty really was a good friend to me, but I'd run out of all the money I received from my husband's estate. I had no way to survive. Your aunt had plenty of money, you know. In fact, she had everything." She sighed and shook her head. "It really wasn't fair. I was tired of being the poor companion." She picked up a napkin from the tea tray and dabbed at her eyes. "You see, some people are simply not as fortunate as others. When I saw that letter, I knew I'd found my salvation. In my attempt to keep it, I panicked. I never took the time to think it out until it was over. The only thing on my mind was that if I wanted to make the letter mine, I had to get Bitty out of the picture. My decision was made in seconds. Bitty climbed up the ladder, and I grabbed a tool from her fireplace set. As she came down, I hit her, although as you suspected, it wasn't hard enough to kill her. If she hadn't fallen off and struck her head, she might have survived." She touched the napkin to her eyes again. "I'm sorry she had to die. I wish it could have been different."

Amos took a step toward her, his face crimson with anger. "You must be insane," he growled. "Other people aren't on this earth just to fulfill your selfish desires. Bitty Flanagan was a person. She had the right to live. It wasn't your choice to take that from her."

"Amos, stay where you are," I said. "Losing your temper now will only help Lila."

He stopped his advance, but he didn't look happy about it.

"Did you know Bitty was still alive when you left her there, Lila?" I asked.

She looked up, obviously startled. "No. I was certain she was dead."

"No. She was just unconscious. She spoke to Isaac when he found her. Would you like to know what she said?"

Lila's narrowed blue eyes sought mine. I looked away. "She said she forgave you."

"Yes, she would, wouldn't she?" There was no more life left in her voice, just resignation. She stood up slowly. "I guess we need to get going, Deputy. May I pack a few things first?"

Amos followed her into her bedroom while Lila got a suitcase and packed the items she thought she might need for a few days. I wasn't certain the jail in Hugoton would allow her to have them, but I didn't feel like saying anything about it and neither did Amos. Lila handed me the box with the letter in it as we were leaving.

Amos drove to the bookstore, pulling up in front and parking so I could get out. He came around to help me navigate over the eternally frozen street. But before I stepped out and accepted his arm, I turned around to face the woman who had killed my aunt. "Lila, it will take me awhile to get rid of the anger I have toward you. I know God will help me with that. But I have to say something to you, even though I don't want to. Even though it goes against everything I'm feeling right now."

Lila stared back at me without emotion.

"I forgive you, Lila," I whispered. "I forgive you because Bitty forgave you. I hope that someday you will be able to forgive yourself."

I got out of the car and took Amos's hand. He helped me up the steps and waited while I unlocked the door.

"Wait a minute," he said, grabbing my shoulders and turning me around to look at him. "That was a brave thing you did," he said. "You've given me the courage to tell you something I should have told you a long time ago."

His eyes misted, and he touched my face with his gloved hand. "When I left Winter Break to live with my father, it wasn't just because I wanted to be with him. It was also because I couldn't be around you anymore. You see, I loved you so much, but you were determined to get out of this town and start a life somewhere else. You didn't care for me the way I wanted you to, so I thought that going away would help me to forget you. It didn't." He smiled and shook his head. "I still love you, Ivy Towers. You're a part of me, and I believe you always will be. Now you're getting ready to make a choice. If you have any feelings for me at all, I hope you'll stay in Winter Break and see if something important develops. If you decide to leave, I'll try to understand. I truly want you to be happy, however it affects me." He let go of me and stepped back. "I wanted you to know how I felt before you made your final decision."

He walked away and got into his car without looking back. I stayed where I was and watched him drive away. Then I sat down on the steps of my aunt's bookstore while the sun began to set upon another frigid day in Winter Break. I stared down the road where he'd disappeared until I was so cold I could no longer feel my feet.

15

Amos didn't return until Tuesday evening. When he finally arrived, I was waiting for him.

"Hey there," he said as he came in the door. Although the sun was peeking through the clouds, another cold front had moved in, bringing wind gusts strong enough to rattle the windows. So instead of being in the single digits, we had plunged a few degrees below zero.

I waited while he struggled out of his heavy winter coat, gloves, hat, and scarf. "So is Lila safely tucked away?" I asked when he had finally unencumbered himself.

"Now there's an interesting question," he said, grinning. He came over to the desk and perched on the edge. "*Lila* is not safely tucked away. However, Rosemary Maxwell is locked up and will most probably stay that way for the rest of her sorry life."

"Rosemary Maxwell? What are you talking about?"

His lopsided smirk reminded me of Alice's Cheshire Cat.

"Remember I told you that someone who killed their spouse was supposed to be hiding out somewhere in Stevens County? Well, it seems that *Lila Hatcher* was a phony name cooked up to cover her tracks. She picked Winter Break because she didn't think anyone would ever find her here. Her real name is Rosemary Maxwell, and she's wanted in Minnesota for killing her husband and taking off with the inheritance. Police didn't suspect her until she disappeared; then they did some investigating and found out that her husband, Edwin, didn't die of a heart attack after all. They've been looking for her ever since she came here. They are quite willing to welcome her back. She's being extradited to Minnesota this week."

"That's amazing," I said. "But how did you find out who she really was?"

Amos shrugged. "The sheriff in Hugoton thought she looked familiar and found her picture on a bulletin from Minnesota. Although she looked a little different, she admitted she was Rosemary Maxwell." He grinned broadly. "And besides putting Rosemary in prison where she belongs, something else good came out of all this.

Since I was 'instrumental' in apprehending their suspect, they're going to equip the office in Winter Break with all the newfangled devices they have available to them in Hugoton."

"And what newfangled devices are we talking about?"

His grin broke into a chuckle. "A computer and a fax machine. It seems that the sheriff realized that if I'd had a chance to see the bulletin for myself, I might have recognized Rosemary much earlier. So now the office in Winter Break is becoming high tech."

He spotted Bitty's list on the desk. "We never did get around to talking about this. I told you I'd figured out something else on this list."

"Oh, you did? And what is that?"

"Number six is . . ."

"Wind clock," I said quickly.

Amos chuckled. "So you got that one, too, huh?"

"That's not all," I said, smiling. "I solved the rest of the entries on the list, *and* I uncovered some new information you might find interesting."

A gust of winter wind shook the windows. "Let's go where it's warm," I said through chattering teeth.

"Okay, but first I have a gift for you."

He grabbed something wrapped in newspaper, lying next to the coatrack. When we were in the sitting room, he unwrapped the package and pulled out a pair of fireplace tongs. They matched the rest of the set perfectly.

"These weren't easy to find," he said as he slid them into the holder with the rest of the implements. "I had to look through three antique stores. Bitty had this set for a long while."

"Thank you, Amos," I said gratefully. "Now it won't be so obvious something is missing. It reminds me . . ."

"I know," he said gently. "I figured as much." He plopped down in the chair across from me. "Now tell me your news."

"Okay, but I have to warn you that I've been quite busy since you left. First of all, I know why Bitty canceled her wedding to Dewey. I also know why he was so upset that Wednesday morning."

"Wow, I'm impressed. Tell me."

"Shortly before Bitty and Dewey planned to set a wedding date, Dewey found out he was diabetic. Even though Lucy told him it was serious, he refused to make the changes she suggested. Aunt Bitty was upset with him and worried about his health. She

303

canceled their plans until he promised to follow all of Lucy's instructions. Wednesday morning, he came flying over to the bookstore to tell her that he'd set an appointment with Lucy so he could get copies of his new diet and start taking his medication. He wasn't really upset. He was just determined to get a date set. Number ten on Bitty's list, the last thing she wrote, was *PT — Ap W?* Remember? I'm convinced it meant *Pastor Taylor — April Wedding?*"

"And how did you find this out?" Amos asked, his eyes wide with surprise.

"Easy. I asked." I grinned at him. "I decided it was time for honesty. Bitty's murder is solved. I was tired of suspecting everyone of something nefarious, so I made a few visits."

"Uh-oh. And who else did you interrogate?"

"I did not interrogate anyone. I *visited* them."

"Sorry, my mistake," Amos said with a laugh. "Okay, who else did you *visit?*"

"Lucy Barber for one," I answered. "We've buried the hatchet. I was right. She was keeping a secret about my aunt."

"A secret? What kind of a secret?" he asked, frowning.

I couldn't help but be a little tickled. His

ego was probably a little bruised because he'd been kept out of the loop. I'd come to the conclusion that Amos was just about as nosy as I was.

"There are a lot of people in Winter Break who either don't have health insurance or don't have enough," I said. "Bitty was paying their bills, Amos. She made Lucy promise not to ever tell anyone what she was doing. That's why Lucy was over here so much, and that's why Bitty wrote *DRL — chk* on the list. She planned to give Dr. Lucy a check to cover medicine for several of the town's residents. Lucy wouldn't allow her to pay her fees when someone couldn't afford to, but she did let Bitty pay for medicines and treatments that she couldn't provide by herself." I shook my head. "Lucy wasn't upset with me at all. She was just worried about her patients. She did come to the bookstore Wednesday morning to pick up the check. When she didn't see my aunt, she left. I suspect that Bitty was lying on the floor where Lucy couldn't see her."

"I'm not surprised about Lucy's anxiety about her patients. I told you that she's a dedicated doctor."

"I know. I'm going to continue the work my aunt started. I've already written her one check, and I intend to give her more when she needs it."

Actually, I didn't tell him everything Lucy confessed to me. She had feelings for Amos, and even though they'd dated a few times, it hadn't taken her long to discover that he was in love with someone else. When I came to town, she figured out that I was the person he couldn't seem to forget. At first she was jealous of me, but eventually she faced the realization that she and Amos had no future. She apologized for her reaction to me, and we mended our broken fences.

"Is that everything, Sherlock?" Amos asked.

I shook my head. "No, not quite. The other day when we were searching the shelves for *The Prince and the Pauper,* I came across an old book about a company that used to make decorative lamps. They've been out of business for a long time. Something about the lamp on the cover made me remember something I'd seen."

"What are you talking about?"

"Elmer Buskin has an old lamp on his desk. I cleaned a little of the dust off of it the night I was there, and I'd planned to go back and finish the job."

"You're not making any sense, Ivy. What does this have to do with anything?"

"Keep your shirt on, smarty-pants," I said,

grinning triumphantly. "I found the same lamp in the book. I borrowed Elmer's computer again and did an Internet search." I paused for dramatic effect. Amos took the bait.

"And . . ."

"And I found that the very same model was recently sold at an auction for forty-five thousand dollars."

Amos was speechless.

"So now Elmer will be able to fix up the funeral home and get on his feet."

"You're an amazing woman, Ivy Towers," Amos said finally. "I swear, I never know what you're going to come up with next."

I shook my head. "It was Great-Aunt Bitty who was amazing, Amos. In fact, I intend to try my best to be more like her. I believe people like Bitty can keep teaching us, even when they're gone, if we listen carefully to the legacy they left behind."

He nodded. "That sounds like an excellent idea. You aunt would be honored to know the impact she's still having in the lives of the people who love her." He leaned back in his chair and stared at the fireplace. "And did you meet with Noel about the store?" He was so quiet I had to strain to hear him. Any feeling of joviality blew out of the room just like the wind that had whipped up such a frenzy outside a few minutes before.

"Yes, I did," I said softly. "And he made me a very good offer."

"How much?" Amos was calm and controlled, but I could see his jaw working furiously.

"He offered me sixty thousand dollars for everything."

"And what did you say?"

"I told him that I couldn't accept. You see, Noel showed me something I hadn't seen before. He told us that running this bookstore was his dream job, but he couldn't afford to do it. I may be a little slow, but I finally figured out he was right. I have a chance to live out my dream job and to be near the man I love. How could I turn that down?"

Amos jumped to his feet and grabbed my hands, pulling me up next to him. The tears in his eyes matched my own.

"I've been praying that God would show me the place he had for me," I said. "I'd started thinking that I didn't belong anywhere. But all the time it was —"

"Standing right in front of you," he finished. His arms surrounded me, and I fell into his embrace.

"That was what Aunt Bitty meant in her

letter," I whispered. "She knew all along where I was supposed to be."

I gazed over his shoulder at the bookstore that was now mine. "There's just one thing," I said.

"What's that?" Amos asked softly.

"How in the world am I going to explain this to my mother?"

Amos laughed. "I have no idea, but we'll figure it out together. We have the rest of our lives."

Right before I kissed him, I said, "Good. That's probably about how long it's going to take."

ALMA PETTIBONE'S
HUCKLEBERRY MUFFINS

3/4 cup butter
1 cup white sugar
1 egg
3/4 cup milk
1 teaspoon vanilla extract
1 3/4 cups sifted all-purpose flour
2 1/2 teaspoons baking powder
1/2 teaspoon salt
1 cup huckleberries
1 tablespoon all-purpose flour

Directions:
Preheat the oven to 400°F (200°C). Grease
15 muffin cups or line with muffin papers.

In a large bowl, cream together the butter
and sugar until smooth. Mix in the egg,
milk, and vanilla until well blended. Combine 1 3/4 cups flour, baking powder, and
salt; stir into the batter until just moistened.
Toss huckleberries with remaining flour to
coat. Then fold them into the batter. Spoon

batter into muffin cups, filling at least 2/3 full.

Bake for 15 minutes in the preheated oven, or until the tops spring back when lightly pressed.

Serve warm with butter or huckleberry jelly!

ABOUT THE AUTHOR

Nancy Mehl's novels are all set in her home state of Kansas. "Although some people think of Kansas as nothing more than flat land and cattle, we really are quite interesting!" she says.

Nancy is a mystery buff who loves the genre and is excited to see more inspirational mysteries becoming available to readers who share her passion. *In the Dead of Winter* combines two of her favorite things — mystery and snow. "Unfortunately, our past several winters have been pretty dry. I enjoy writing fiction because I can make it snow as much as I want!"

Besides writing, she is also a popular book reviewer. She has reviewed for the Charlotte Austin Review, MyShelf.com, Midwest Book Review, and the Wichita Eagle.

Nancy works for the City of Wichita, assisting low-income seniors and the disabled. Her volunteer group, Wichita Homebound

Outreach, seeks to demonstrate the love of God to special people who need to know that someone cares.

She lives in Wichita, Kansas, with her husband of thirty-five years, Norman. Her son, Danny, is a graphic designer who has designed several of her book covers. They attend World of Life Church. Her Web site is www.nancymehl.com.